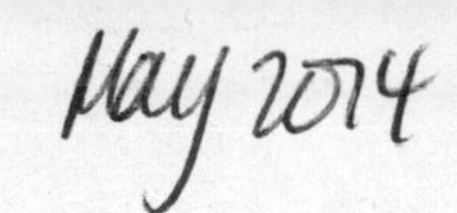

Praise for Frank Lentricchia and
THE ACCIDENTAL PALLBEARER

"Frank Lentricchia's new novel ranks as entertainment of a high order—funny, fast-moving, and hot-blooded. It's also the kind of novel that will appeal to readers who like their fiction to carry depth and range."
—DON DELILLO

"Bravissimo!" **—LISA SCOTTOLINE, AUTHOR OF *ACCUSED***

"*The Accidental Pallbearer* is a brilliant piece of fiction, and a page-turner to boot, able to stand shoulder to shoulder with the best writing in America today."
—JAY PARINI

"*The Accidental Pallbearer* deserves to be read alongside the best literary detective fiction of our time. Lentricchia's protagonist is the antihero par excellence—you can't put him down, either physically or emotionally."
—JOHN R. MACARTHUR, PUBLISHER, *HARPER'S*

"Gripping, complex ... Utica here functions much as the Swedish town Ystad does for Henning Mankell in his books about Wallander ... An excellent start for these Eliot Conte books. Can't wait for the next one—and the cable-TV series."
—THE PHILADELPHIA INQUIRER

"Full of bits and pieces of authentic Utica history, altered and molded into a totally fictional story that is fast-paced and thrilling, scene after scene. It has the hard-bitten diction and action of 'Film Noir.' "
—THE UTICA OBSERVER-DISPATCH

"There's a Quentin Tarantino masculinity to this story of a private investigator known for solving knotty problems in not-quite-lawful ways." **—*THE CHARLOTTE OBSERVER***

"If you like your crime very noir, very hard-boiled and very American, then this is the novel for you." **—*THE TELEGRAPH* (LONDON)**

"Lentricchia captures the feel of upstate New York (Richard Russo territory) and of Italian American culture within a familiar genre, with predictable grit and wit." **—*BOOKLIST***

"The terrific writing, clever plots, bleak humor, and colorful characters recommend this to fans of gritty noir crime fiction."
—*LIBRARY JOURNAL* (STARRED REVIEW)

THE DOG KILLER OF UTICA

ALSO BY FRANK LENTRICCHIA

The Accidental Pallbearer
The Portable Lentricchia
The Sadness of Antonioni
The Italian Actress
The Book of Ruth
Lucchesi and The Whale
The Music of the Inferno
Johnny Critelli
The Knifemen
The Edge of Night (memoir/fiction)

FRANK LENTRICCHIA

THE DOG KILLER OF UTICA

Special thanks to Jeff Jackson, for always-on-target advice, and a tip of the hat to John R. MacArthur for his reporting on the Utica Homeland Security pork barrel in his book *The Outrageous Barriers to Democracy in America.*

MELVILLE INTERNATIONAL CRIME

THE DOG KILLER OF UTICA

First Melville House Printing: April 2014

Melville House Publishing
145 Plymouth Street
Brooklyn, NY 11201
and
8 Blackstock Mews
Islington
London N4 2BT

mhpbooks.com facebook.com/mhpbooks @melvillehouse

ISBN: 978-1-61219-337-3

Manufactured in the United States of America
1 3 5 7 9 10 8 6 4 2

A catalog record for this book is available
from the Library of Congress.

For Gene Nassar and Bob Cimbalo
With a salute to the guys at Toma's
1160 Mohawk Street
Utica, New York

THE KING OF MARY STREET

They appeared ten years ago in the dead of winter, next door to Eliot Conte on Mary Street—those vivid Mexican immigrants, Florencio and Elvira Moreno and their three-year-old son, whom they had named Angel. They came long after Conte had lost his children on the West Coast in a vicious divorce and moved back to Utica, New York—where, broke in spirit and in pocket, he was sustained by his politically powerful father's unstinting generosity. Conte was living alone. He was well past fifty. He was pursuing with noteworthy success a career in alcoholism and working as a private investigator, the practice of which was yielding the usual paltry and repulsive business. And so it was that he had much time on his hands to sit at home, pale-skinned while the sun shone, reading literary classics and revising his thirty-year-old UCLA master's thesis on Herman Melville, with unreasonable thoughts of publication. Melville—the writer whose vision seemed to tell Conte, the quietly godless Conte, that nothing had ever mattered in the long run, and nothing ever would. Just why godless Conte was drawn to the immigrants next door he could never have said. Perhaps the Moreno family was something, rather than nothing, for the long run. Perhaps the Moreno family would prove Melville to be wrong, though Eliot Conte—a big man of violent impulse—doubted it.

One warm Sunday morning late in their first American spring, Conte watched secretly from a back window as the burly and bare-chested Florencio Moreno collected the rags, the frying pan without a handle, the pieces of old iron, the shards of glass, and the deteriorated corpse of a cat before commencing to turn over the earth in his backyard and planting tomatoes, lettuce, pole beans, cucumbers, and herbs. Suddenly Conte found himself pulled irresistibly outdoors into the sun. From the other side of the fence in his yard he motioned to Florencio and said that he, who'd never planted anything, would like to tear down the fence that he had paid handsomely to install and would Florencio like to help? Together they could make one big son of a gun of a garden. Conte did not know what possessed him to make such a proposition. Florencio quickly agreed and they tore down the fence with manly exuberance, though in the beginning the plants on Florencio's side did better by far than those on Conte's side. Of course, Conte could not himself consume all that grew on his side and he encouraged Florencio to take whatever he wanted, whenever he felt the need. Even so, there was too much for both of them, so they decided to give away a portion of their great harvest to neighbors, who were stunned, but grateful.

There was a time, more than fifty years ago, when all the backyards of Mary Street bloomed with cultivated plenty, especially those on the 1300 block, where Conte and the Morenos lived, but many of the children of the original Mary Street immigrant Italians, not to mention the grandchildren, had no time for gardens and grapevines, as they worked assiduously on their American lives and dreamed of what they called freedom, in California, while all gardens, all grapevines, disappeared.

Florencio soon cured the stunted earth on Conte's side and the garden from one end to the other became uniformly rich and dense with good things, which nothing in the supermarkets could ever match. Conte's gargantuan salads required neither salt nor pepper and only a hint of olive oil because under Florencio's magical husbandry the earth itself had infused those flavors and in the third spring and summer of cooperative gardening, Conte—ruddy complected from outdoor labor—became almost as good as Florencio, who had taught him to coax abundance from begrudging backyard dirt.

Then one fateful evening in damp and drizzly November, as Conte reread *Moby-Dick* for the twelfth time, Elvira in distress knocked on his door. Her brother-in-law, who lived in Syracuse, had suffered a heart attack and was it possible that Señor Conte could watch their son, now six, while she and Florencio went to Syracuse for a few hours? He would go to sleep soon, angel that he was, and give no trouble, she promised. Conte said, Yes, of course, and took his *Moby-Dick* with him. While the child slept, he'd resume his peculiarly pleasurable meditation on Melville's nameless terror.

Naturally, the presence in his room of this giant American from next door who was said to eat giant salads excited the child, and deferred his sleep, and Conte didn't know what to do. The boy, who'd learned English in a jiffy after only a year and a half of schooling, asked for a story. Conte replied, Where are your storybooks? The boy said, with an impish look, We have none. My parents make them up. So Conte tried to make one up, but this man who loved the stories of great writers was himself no storyteller. At a loss, and afraid of failing the boy, he decided to tell a story that his own father had told him of a man who died before Conte was born. A man known as The King of Mary Street. The boy responded, *El Rey de Calle Maria!* Even at six, the boy had a presence, a bearing, an alertness that caused Conte to believe, absurdly, but inescapably, that he was in the company of an equal.

He started haltingly, unsure of himself, as he remembered his father telling it to him when he was the boy's age. If only he could have recorded his father's telling with its dramatic fluctuations of tone, its long seamless rhythms, and the rich detail of a world he'd never seen—the world of The King of Mary Street, who became known as The King only after death, Conte said, whose name was Tomaso, who lived at 1303 Mary—across the street and down the block almost to Bacon. (Bacon and eggs! shouts the boy.) When he was the same age as your father is now, in 1918, Tomaso planted a cherry tree in his backyard, a sapling of two feet, and all around that sapling he planted a garden. The sapling grew into a normal-sized cherry tree—it took fifteen years, until Tomaso was no longer young, in the heart of the Great Depression. Eighteen feet high, it was, and fruitful, as cherry trees are, every other year. Tomaso knew trees as well as he knew the body of his wife. (The boy grins.) He knew that he must not allow that tree to go beyond itself, because its boughs would become too heavy and peel off the trunk in a disaster and the tree would die a slow and terrible death, as it destroyed the garden beneath itself, but Tomaso let it grow anyway against all reason and saw it in his dreams producing at great height enough cherries to feed all of Mary Street should another time come, as surely it would, when all of Mary Street would again be poor and hungry. Eighteen feet. Twenty. Twenty-five. By 1948, the Tree was forty-five feet high. It was higher than the house. It was wider than the backyard. The great boughs reached over into the neighbors' yards, who did not mind. Some said that Tomaso's youngest and most mischievous son (the boy claps his hands) walked the greatest of all the Tree's boughs into a yard three blocks away in order to taunt that neighbor's dog who barked all night and made Tomaso curse a curse so obscene that I will not translate it. (The boy is disappointed.) The Tree loomed over the block. The Tree loomed over lower East Utica. The Tree loomed over the city.

Then one winter night the Tree grew weary of its greatness and desired never again to awaken in spring, because the Tree did not want to face another July when Tomaso and his sons and sons-in-law picked all the cherries, as they cursed the robins who fought them for their fair share—the burly men all the while talking amongst themselves high up inside the Tree and disturbing the Tree's peaceful inner life. Cherries big like golf balls. Cherries like baseballs. Cherries like soccer balls. Conte was on his own, now, adding to his father's telling, having a good time as he forgot that in the long run nothing ever mattered, and that all good things must come to an end.

The great boughs began to slowly peel away, which is what they wanted to do, so Tomaso put two-by-sixteens up under their formidable asses to keep them from doing what they wanted to do, but they kept on peeling away and so he bought many long strong black belts and tied them one bough to the other, so that the Tree's interior was elaborately criss-crossed with black belts and couldn't do what it wanted to do, which was to die. Terrible oozing gashes appeared where the great boughs joined the trunk and all along the trunk itself and so he, Tomaso, poured actual cement into the gashes to defeat bugs and disease, and suddenly the Tree changed its mind. It began to entertain ideas of an eternal life. It would suffer, it decided, the troubles of July and those fools, those burly men who picked.

And so it went, every other summer, Tomaso and sons and sons-in-law carrying their heavy sagging baskets in to Natalina, Tomaso's small, fierce wife—pouring basket after basket into a golden bowl—pouring all through July—pouring to the brim—the golden bowl never overflowing no matter how much was poured and Natalina and her daughters and daughters-in-law cooked, preserved, and canned and gave hundreds of pounds to the family and the neighbors and the blessed golden bowl remained full of sweet cherries to the brim, no matter how much was taken out.

The Great Tree would not die a natural death, but Tomaso and Natalina did, and soon after the sons and sons-in-law and the daughters and daughters-in-law lost all interest in the Tree. The house at 1303 Mary Street was sold to a politician, who cut the Tree down and blacktopped the garden. The little Moreno boy, struggling now against The Sandman, wanted to know where Tomaso and Natalina were. He wanted to see them. He wanted to know what happened to the golden bowl. He wanted one for his mother. He wanted to see the Tree before it was cut down. Over and over he asked Conte, What was the name of that barking dog? Tell me the dog's name or I'll get mad at you. Conte, at a loss, but seeing that sleep was at last capturing the boy, whispered, I don't know, and the boy whispered, Who knows, señor, and fell fast asleep.

Then Conte arose from the side of the bed where he'd been sitting and walked out to the living room, where he picked up *Moby-Dick* and sat in a comfortable chair to resume his twelfth rereading, but he couldn't do it. Instead, he looked for and found a piece of blank paper and a pencil and made a long list of names for the barking dog. He settled on: *Il Diavolo della Strada Maria*. The Devil of Mary Street. Then, recalling the little bit of Spanish he'd learned in his California days, he wrote: *El Diablo de Calle Maria*, which is what he would tell the boy when he saw him again. He hoped it would be soon—he hoped it would be very soon.

Years later, when the Moreno child is twelve, the two daughters that Conte had lost in a vicious divorce on the West Coast are murdered—to all appearances either by his ex-wife, Nancy, or her husband, Ralph, or both, but no charges were filed, and the long-absent father raced from his grief with legs of stone, while in the grip of his desire for revenge.

THE PRESENT

CHAPTER 1

He's pulled up in panic from the world of a recurring nightmare—at 5:00 A.M. Eliot Conte lurches heavily to the other side of the bed—where she is not—where he inhales, thinks he inhales, her fragrance—brooding now on this day of their six-month anniversary—six months to the day that Catherine Cruz had resigned her position as detective in the Troy, New York, Police Department and moved to Utica to assume the same post under Chief of Police Antonio Robinson, Conte's all-but-in-blood African-American brother—six months since that night when she moved into the house at 1318 Mary Street, in Utica's former East Side Italian-American fortress, and whispered in his bed thrilling words he'd never before heard—and yet, and yet, absurdly, deep into that first night and weekly thereafter (he fears forever thereafter), nightmares of unrequitable longing (his) for unreachable remoteness (hers), in a landscape whose sole promise of redemption is death.

5:30, sipping a second double-shot espresso in the kitchen, when he hears the clock radio awaken to the swollen bass-baritone of Anthony V. Senzalma, intoning his daily dark forewarnings of "creeping Sharia law," "the radical homosexual agenda," and the "Kenyan socialist usurping the White

House." Conte strides to the bedroom, turns off the radio, sheds his pajama top and bottoms, and crawls under the covers on her side of the bed—seeking the embrace of her absent presence as he reaches for his fading rationality, as he reminds himself that she'd gone yesterday to Troy only for a quick trip, that's all it was, and would return later today, possibly tomorrow morning—no later than that. To Troy to attend to the most recent of the self-inflicted crises of her twenty-three-year-old daughter, which she'll resolve, quickly, by writing a check. That's all it was. While there, if she had time, she'd stop in to see her former partner, their mutual pal, Detective Robert Rintrona.

"Give Bobby my regards if you see him," he'd said, as she, looking her blazing best, got into the car.

"Any special message for Bobby?"

"Tell him not to be concerned about a thing."

She looks sharply at him, "Concerned? What could Bobby possibly be concerned about? Unless it's the latest inadequate replacement for the King of the High Cs?"

He puts his guard back up with a smile. He touches her shoulder and withholds the truth he'd withheld from her for a year: "That's it exactly, Ms. Cruz. The latest Pavarotti imposter. That's all I had in mind."

On that bitter mid-December Sunday morning, in this town on life support, which calls itself The Gateway to the Adirondacks, she replies, "One of these days, Mr. Conte, you'll tell me the secret. Or else—pow! pow!—you're dead," as she mimes shooting him, then speeds off to the Thruway exit in North Utica for the eighty-mile ride down to Troy.

6:15, he's shoving open with unnecessary force the glass

door to POWER UP!, the studio for personal training adjacent to the northern edge of Utica College's campus, where he's been a regular, three times per week, for the last nine months, beginning a month after he'd suffered a severe beating at the hands of an "unknown assailant" (as it was phrased in the *Observer-Dispatch*), whose identity Conte was certain of. (It was Ralph, who'd come east after Nancy had received Eliot's letter accusing Ralph of sexually abusing his girls.) He had revealed the assailant's identity only to Antonio Robinson, who promised to keep "this thing between ourselves, as our good father taught us, may his soul rest in peace." Robinson then added, coldly, "Eventually you make the long-delayed journey to the West Coast and deliver life-changing gifts to your ex and this cunt Ralph Norwald, who abused your kids. Deliver them, soon, El, from life to the other side, where they sent your daughters." Conte replies softly, without affect, "Emily and Rosalind."

The studio opens at 6:30, but his trainer arrives at 5:45 for his own daily workout and Conte comes eagerly fifteen minutes in advance of his 6:30 appointment to watch Kyle Torvald in the last jaw-dropping phase of his routine: fifty strict pull-ups and a fifty-first at the top of which Kyle actually muscles himself up and over the bar—this morning bellowing "Con-TEEEEEE"—dropping to the floor, palms up: "In the dog house? Where's our fair lady? Where is Detective Catherine Cruuuuuz?"

In this place of violent manly exertion, Conte finds a curious tranquility, as if he'd entered the enclosing warmth of an unfailingly supportive home. No pangs, here, of physical inadequacy, not a trace of macho thrust and parry, except in parodic mockery, never a hint of the bloody male imperative, except once, at the first interview, when Kyle—ex-paratrooper with a problematic back—in response to Conte's question, "What's a reasonable fitness goal for a guy my age?" replies with a wink, "When you take off your shirt, big guy, you look like you might, and likely will, sooner or later, kill somebody." Kyle Torvald stands 5'10" at 160 pounds, a fair blond of Scandinavian descent and delicately chiseled handsomeness, beside Eliot Conte's 6'3", 220, and all southern Italian shadow.

Kyle says (with glee), "Addicted to breathing? I can fix that. Get on the rower and give me two thousand meters, all out, and vomit! Vomit your guts!—quick, down on the floor, forty push-ups, crack your spine!—quick! Quick! Bench two hundred pounds to muscle failure—die slowly!—burst your clotted chest!—give me one hundred squats in one hundred seconds—no resting, Conte!—pull that five-hundred-pound sled back and forth the length of the floor and stop making those noises! Did I see you eye-fuck the clock? Would you like the Suicide Stairs? Hurry! Hurry! Slam that thirty-pound medicine ball, not on the floor but through it, twenty times, penetrate that floor, Conte, rape it hard and explode your evil heart and balls."

"Good work," Kyle says, the only compliment he ever gives, and that not often, as he extends his hand to help his spent trainee off the floor, while startling him with an offer (a first) to go to breakfast "on me."

Conte, on his feet, barely, manages, "You're free?"

"Congressman Kingwood canceled his 7:00, Anthony Senzalma his 7:30. Why, you may ask? Because these right-wing homophobes decided to suck each other off. I have nothing at 8:00. Let's go, big fella. Or do you need an ambulance?"

Kohler's For Breakfast (since 1947), in the ex-Polish enclave on the West Side, a memory of the Utica that was. Front room of a one-family house. Five tables, worn carpeted floor, actual flowers in all seasons, pictures of old-time political bosses. Mama cooks. Papa waits: soft-boiled eggs, cream of wheat and sliced banana, coffee and pastries—Kyle insists on the sweets "because if you don't once in a while, the craving pushes you into a zone of violence." Conte, who needs no excuse, replies, "Let's order the Napoleons for the road and save the violence for another day."

"Which day?"

(Pause.)

"Tomorrow."

"Now that you teach at the college, ever miss your private dick work?"

"No."

"Not even a little?"

"No."

"Good guy bad guy thrill of the hunt?"

"Good guy? What's that?"

"You, Eliot."

"Coming on to me, Kyle?"

"I'm contemplating coming on to Catherine."

"You're gay—have you forgotten?"

"Skin deep, Prof, just skin deep."

(Conte thinks of her skin, the feel of it. He smiles weakly.)

"Out of curiosity, Conte, do you and Catherine, in your spare time, hunt the guy who did the damage to your body?

When you came to see me two weeks after it happened, you still looked pretty ugly. How did she handle it? I'm her, I want to kill the guy."

Eliot nods.

"You know who did it, don't you?"

Eliot nods.

"And why."

Eliot nods.

"Has to do with your kids who were …"

Eliot nods.

"What are you going to do about it?"

Eliot stares.

Kyle waves over George Kohler, orders two Napoleons to go, then says, "Me? I'm merely a man of physical culture who can't go toe-to-toe at your psychological level. Aside from the incomparable Catherine, who can?"

"Kyle?"

"I'm here, Eliot."

"Neither can I."

Catherine Cruz in Troy the previous day had done what Conte imagined she'd do. Hugged her daughter, took her to dinner, picked up the clothes-strewn apartment, washed and put away the sink-clogging, days-old dirty dishes, wiped down every dust-laden surface while Miranda sat in observance, in sullen stupor, waiting for her mother to perform the ultimate act of commiseration by writing a more-than-generous check. That night, Catherine sleeps badly on Miranda's couch.

Next morning, while Conte is put through his brutalizing

paces, Catherine awakes in time to hear the apartment door close and her daughter slink out to score whatever it was that made her minimal life possible. Catherine falls in despair immediately back to a trouble-free sleep of escape, to be startled awake two hours later by an unnaturally exuberant "Good morning! *Mi madre!*" Against all reason she's washed over by memories of Miranda's childhood innocence, magically resuscitated by this transparently sweet apparition who walks back into the apartment. Catherine Cruz is torn asunder by the conspiring parties of joy, guilt, and sadness without bottom.

Late that morning, she pulls away from the curb, her radio tuned to FM Albany. When nearing the Thruway entrance, a crushing bulletin: "*This just in. Longtime Troy favorite, respected detective, and Christmas Day Parade Santa Claus, Robert Rintrona, is reported to be in grave condition at Saint Jude's Hospital after suffering three gunshot wounds in the driveway of his west Troy home, early this morning. Details and updates at the top of the hour. And now back to our regularly scheduled program, and Act Two of Verdi's* Un Ballo in Maschera, *a great love of the detective's, as we are told.*"

She turns back, racing over the speed limit toward Saint Jude—the hospital and the Saint himself.

The heavy workout and even heavier breakfast make it difficult for Conte to stay awake as he drives across town to Mary Street, where he takes a long, hot shower, somehow resists the urge to try Catherine on her cell, then curls up on the couch and sleeps for an hour. Awake, reviews his notes for his last presentation of the semester, metaphysical nihilism in *Moby-Dick*, when he's rescued from Melville's terror by the desk phone.

"Eliot."

"Where are you? Almost home?"

"On the Thruway."

"When will you be home?"

"About an hour."

"Drive safely."

"I always drive safely."

"Miss me, Catherine?"

"Yes."

"Watch out for bad drivers. They're the ones who—"

"I'll try."

"Really watch out."

"I'll try."

"No need to rush."

"No."

"Kyle asked after you. He has a thing for you, even though he's gay. He says he's only gay at the surface."

"Eliot, are you sitting or standing?"

"What's that supposed to—?"

"Eliot. Sitting or standing?"

"Standing. Christ, Catherine."

"You should sit."

"What happened? Are you—?"

"Nothing. I'm fine."

"Miranda?"

"No."

"Bobby Rintro—?"

"Bobby was shot."

"They killed Bobby?" (Coldly.)

"He's still alive. Why did you say 'they'?"

"How bad?" (Coldly.)

"Bad."

"Where? When?"

"Walking his dog this morning in his pajamas and robe and Santa hat. In front of the house. Maureen was still asleep. Three times."

"Not the head. Don't tell me—"

(Conte breaks down. She thinks it'll never end.)

"Shoulder. Neck. Missed the artery. Chest ... They have grave concern ... Lung damage. The trauma surgeon says a decent recovery is possible."

"What is decent supposed to mean? Fifty-fifty chance of dying?"

"He never lost consciousness until they put him under."

(Silence.)

"Are you there, Eliot?"

"Did you see Maureen?"

"No."

"Did you talk to the responding officers?"

"Patrolmen Joe Dominguez and Neal Brady."

"Bobby could still talk?"

"He said an upstate plate. Likely Utica."

"He'll survive?"

"Bobby was coughing blood. Brady said drowning in his own—"

"Don't say it. I'll drive down."

"No point. No one outside Maureen and the kids for

several days. Dominguez thinks he said something about Eddie or Ellie or something. He couldn't quite get it. 'Tell Eddie or Ellie that it finally—' "

"Finally? Finally what?"

" 'Tell Eddie or Ellie that it finally—' That's all they got. 'That it finally—' "

(Long silence.)

"Eliot, are you still there?"

"You shouldn't be talking and driving."

"I'll be home soon."

"I'll be at class when you—I'll cancel."

"Don't. We'll talk after."

"Which hospital?"

"Saint Jude. Albany."

"Patron saint of lost causes."

"Yes, Eliot."

One call from Troy and Conte's dragged back into the past. Can he keep the truth from her? If he can't, he's sure he'll lose her. And if he can—what then? He's certain beyond a reasonable doubt that Bobby Rintrona's assailant was Antonio Robinson, and that he's next on the hit list.

Can't prepare—head aswim—will stick closely to his notes. State what he believes to be the book's master theme: the pull of the earth's enchanting surfaces, the engrossing beauty of surfaces and the opposing pull, the self-annihilating dive beneath to find the meaning of ultimate things, where there are no things, and Melville's obsessive key words for what lies beneath the surface. He'll just list the words. He'll repeat them slowly, that's what he'll do.

BLANK
INDEFINITE
IMMEASURABLE
NAMELESS
UNNAMEABLE
PHANTOM
UNDISCOVERABLE
UNIMAGINABLE
INCOMMUNICABLE
INSUFFERABLE
NOTHING

He'll linger on *unimaginable.* Ask them to take it literally. You can't make an image of it. Stay home at the enchanting surface. The spouse. The child. The backyard garden. Squeeze the hands of all brothers and sisters—never forgetting those with whom we do not share blood. The rest is insufferable. He guessed he had at best twenty minutes' worth in him.

The class went the full two and a half hours. Conte lost in a book. Conte happy. Because he felt—as Saint Anthony says we feel in perfect prayer—that he did not exist at all.

CHAPTER 2

4:30, class out and Conte exists again—returned unhappily to himself—walking fast toward the parking lot accompanied by his strongest student, Mirko Ivanovic—apolitical son of Bosnian Muslims who had carried their child when he was three to America's promised land (Utica!) only to see him grow up into a fanatical English major. Mirko's parents would have preferred that he prepare himself for the sanctioned thievery of Big Business, but they were good parents, above all they were good, who would not impose their will, so they nursed their desires in silent prayer, and in secret stupefaction marveled that this exceptionally bright son of theirs could be enthralled by the books of a long-dead American, who in his lifetime achieved great commercial and critical disasters. With disturbing adulation, in his parents' speechless presence, no less, the devilish Mirko routinely refers to the writer of difficult storybooks as Muhammad Melville.

Diminutive Mirko jogs now to keep pace with his powerfully striding giant of a teacher, as he, Mirko, extends between quick breaths an invitation to attend an interfaith gathering on Sunday at the new mosque in East Utica—at Mary and Albany—a short walk from your house—professor—just a getting to know your—a getting to know your Muslim neighbors—kind of thing—special coffee—divine pastries baked by our ch-chaste—our chaste—mothers and sisters—Conte struggling all the while with a brutal image that has seized the center of his mind, of Robert Rintrona shot down in the street and drowning in his own blood. They reach the car. A sudden flurry of snow, cutting wind. The ever-polite Conte suppresses his impatience to get home, where Catherine Cruz will greet him with perhaps hopeful news. He accepts the invitation. Mirko says "Inshallah" with a curious trace of sadness, or is it fatality?

It's Monday, his and Catherine's date night, their eat-out night, but Conte cannot imagine eating, in or out. What he imagines in vivid detail is a few triple Johnnie Walker Blacks, no ice. He needs to call his sponsor. Needs to go to a meeting. He's driving along the Parkway—elevated terrain directly south of his home in lower East Utica. The Parkway, site of a number of Utica's most expensive homes, now bordering dangerous territory. Conte's vision of triple Johnnie Walkers is penetrated by the sirens of fire trucks, ambulances, police cruisers. The all too familiar sounds emanate from just below the Parkway, in the Cornhill section of white flight, which the Irish, the Germans, the Jews—three versions of middle-class pretension—fled long ago, to be replaced by honest working-class blacks and their cancerous parasites from the black criminal class—the drug dealers, the prostitutes, the pimps, and the arsonists who set fire to rundown two- and three-family houses, sometimes on behalf of slum lords, sometimes just for the hell of it. Conte thinks of the clamor of those sirens as the music of Utica's inferno.

He turns off the Parkway, cuts down to the Cornhill

district on Seymour Ave.—the street where she once lived and where he would cruise in high school days in hopes of seeing her for whom he carried a torch—departed years ago to Las Vegas, married to a lout and womanizer. The house of her youth and beauty is ablaze. Another on Dudley Ave., also ablaze. Anthony V. Senzalma had called Cornhill the "Zone of Black Fire" on his talk show and in an Op-Ed he'd written for the *Observer-Dispatch* that brought him useful death threats. (Conte needs to go to a meeting.) He's weaving his way around cordoned-off, smoke-filled streets of flashing lights and burly men at labor made more difficult, and dangerous, by a strong wind that jumps the fire to two other houses on Brinkerhoff. At last he reaches Freddy Barbone's liquor store on Mohawk at South Street, where he hasn't appeared for a year, since the day before he entered The Program in order to become, as they say, a friend of Bill Wilson.

Freddy steps out from behind the cash register with a booming "Hey! Hey! Johnnie W! Mr. Johnnie Walker himself is back! For some Black!" Throwing his arms wide as he approaches Conte for a hug. Conte freezes, arms at his side, dead-faced. Freddy freezes too, with a look of fear, two feet away, his arms still out. (Rumors of Conte's unpredictable explosions of volcanic rage have reached his ears.) A comic moment, not enjoyed by either actor.

"Long time no see, Eliot," embarrassed, retreating behind the cash register. "Ever get the Mass card I sent when your great father passed? Because I never heard from you."

"Because I never got it."

Because Freddy had not sent a Mass card. Because why

would he? Because while it was always important to make gestures of respect to the powerful father when he was alive, once the old fuck was dead Freddy calculated the profit and the loss and concluded why waste the time and cash on this booze-bag loser of a son, this joke of a private dick who while the father was alive, they say, made money taking secret and bribe-worthy photos of extramarital blow jobs. Freddy's contempt was only confirmed when he'd heard that Conte had retired his practice as a private investigator, was living easy off the inheritance and teaching part-time at the college in the English department. Literature teaching? Freddy cannot imagine anything resembling *more* the act of whacking off furiously in the doorless stall of a public toilet.

Barbone had assumed for the last year that Conte had tried to kick the habit, but clearly he failed, this pathetic bastard, and now here he is and Freddy, though Conte has yet to make a request, is bagging a fifth of Eliot's poison of choice and refusing payment.

"Hey! No way, my friend!"

Conte puts his credit card on the counter, saying not a word.

Freddy, forcing a snort, says "What are you going to do, detective? If I don't accept it? Shoot me? You can pay for the next one."

Conte says nothing.

Freddy runs the credit card, Conte signs.

Freddy, brightening, "I hope to see you again soon because the pleasure of your company is all mine. Know what I got under here, Eliot?" He points to the counter. "Fuckin' niggers come here with their gasoline, they find out what I got under here. By the way, ever shoot anyone?"

Eliot pulls up to 1318 Mary to find Catherine Cruz standing on the front porch, shivering in a lightweight sweater, smoking, who had quit in solidarity a year ago on the day she'd accompanied him to an open meeting where he qualified: "I'm Eliot. I'm an alcoholic." He approaches carrying his Johnnie Walker in the brown bag with Barbone's Booze emblazed on it in red. She flips the cigarette into the gathering snowstorm. They go in. Without a word. He's convinced: Bobby is dead. She'd received a call from an ex-colleague in Troy with connections to the spokesman at Saint Jude. Then she'd bought a pack, and who would blame her, and now he'll join her in resumed addiction and drink with impunity because Bobby is dead. She leads him into the kitchen where the table is set and the aroma from a pizza box from Napoli's fills the room.

She, pointing to the bag, "That's the store on Mohawk and South, northeast corner. Correct?"

Bobby's gone—she's avoiding breaking the news: "What's the difference where I bought it?"

"My partner and I stop in there once in a while to warn Freddy not to sell to minors. Don Belmonte, you know Don, he says he's almost willing to pay to have Freddy burned down. Don was close to your father, he tells me."

(They back away from each other to opposite ends of the kitchen.)

"Catherine."

"Yes?"

"Stop this game."

"Going to drink, Eliot?"

"I earned it, same way you earned that cigarette."

"Meaning?"

Conte does not reply.

"That stuff sends you deeper into depression."

"Doesn't matter anymore."

"Why?"

"Enough."

He takes the bottle out of the bag: "Go ahead, light up again while I pour myself a big one."

"I bought the pack. I threw away nineteen and kept the one you saw. That's it."

"Let's figure this out in fairness to both of our sad sides. I pour out one shot—like this. I dump the rest down the sink—like this. Going going gone. I knock back this shot but not before you go fetch the butt, light up, and inhale deeply. Then we get down on our knees and pray for the repose of his eternal soul."

She walks over. Puts her arms around him. He's aroused. She puts her hand on his crotch: "Bobby is alive and so is this thing in my hand. Listen: I'm weaker than you. You find that hard to believe, I know. I smoked. You don't have to match me with that shot glass."

"Don't lie to me, Catherine."

"In tough shape, El, but he'll pull through, with what consequences we don't yet know. He's alive. You can visit in a few days. You will see him again. You two will talk about pirated Pavarotti gems."

"Bobby didn't die?"

"Bobby didn't die."

He pours the shot into the sink. Sits, heavily, suddenly exhausted, wanting to go to bed for a week: "At least he didn't die."

(Long pause.)

"At least, El?"

No response.

"At least? I don't get that."

"I'm hungry. Tell you after we eat."

"Tell me now. At *least*? I don't get that."

"After we eat. Tell me about Bobby's situation while I tear into this."

(Long pause. Conte is eating. Fast. She doesn't eat.)

"The shoulder wound. The bullet passed through. He'll likely have permanent trouble with range of motion with that arm, but—"

Conte with a mouthful: "Since he isn't a big league pitcher, who cares?"

"Yeah, El."

"Sweetheart, this isn't pizza as you always call it. It's tomato pie. Say tomato pie."

"The neck wound was superficial despite the heavy bleeding and—"

"According to a local historian and writer who knows everything, you know Gene? Tomato pie is a Utica invention. 1914. O'Scugnizzo Pizzeria. The owner was the Neapolitan inventor of tomato pie in this country. Some claim an earlier, Trenton, New Jersey origin, but Gene disputes the Jersey pretender's claim. Eugeno—"

"Eliot."

"Eugeno Burlino was the original owner of O'Scugnizzo Pizzeria."

(Extended silence while he eats.)

"El. Where are you? Come back."

"The meaning of O'Scugnizzo is embedded in nineteenth-century dialect and the culture of the poor. It means —"

"Okay. I'll play. O'Scugnizzo on Bleecker. Don and I go there for a slice once in a while, midafternoon."

"You and Don Belmonte, that beautiful mountain of a man, pushing seventy, or I'd be jealous. Continue, please. The fucking medical report."

"The lung shot. That's the problem. Caused something according to my source inside Saint Jude which he called a *tension pneumothorax*. Don't ask. It's dramatic is all I know. The wounded lung fills up with too much air like a big balloon. It keeps inflating and inflating. Putting pressure on all the structures around the lung. Blood vessels get compressed. The trachea gets shoved to the side. The heart gets shoved to the side. Blood can't flow normally." (Conte continues eating.) "Bobby goes into shock. Without emergency treatment, intubation, surgery, he dies in an hour or so." (Conte wipes his mouth. Takes another piece.) "They open him up and they save him. He'll live but he almost—"

"There's twenty-five pieces in this box. I've scarfed four to your zero. More Diet Coke?"

She reaches across, takes his hand. Says, quietly, "He'll be okay. Will you?"

"Anything is possible."

"They think in surgery they may have damaged something

called the laryngeal something-or-other nerve. It will cause significant hoarseness. Nerves are tricky. It might never fully heal."

"Which makes him an even more colorful guy. The routine obscenities sound even dirtier."

(They relax, a little.)

"Eat, Catherine."

She nibbles. She says, "I've listened to perp talk for too long. *At least he's alive*? I'm going to take a big leap here. You knew for some time that Bobby was in danger. This was not some pissed off guy he once helped put away in Troy. This is a guy hired to do assassination. A Utica plate, presumably. You knew this was coming, didn't you? Which is why you said *they* killed him. 'Tell Eddie or Ellie that it finally,' is what Patrolman Dominguez heard."

He won't look at her. Pushes his plate aside. Says, "What Bobby was trying to say was tell Eliot that what he feared for a year has finally happened. I didn't know it was coming—I feared it was."

The phone rings in the front room. The answering machine: "El, it's me. Call me back soon. Very soon."

She says, "Sounds like Chief Robinson."

"I'm ready to tell you the story."

"Let's sit on the couch. I want to be close."

"Right here," he says.

The answering machine again: "I know you're jumping to conclusions about what happened to your pal down there."

Conte walks slowly to the phone. Begins to call. Hangs up. Picks up the receiver, hesitates, then calls: "Come over later. Let's say at eight. Have you lost common sense? This is a conversation that can't be had on the phone. Catherine will be out for a couple of hours." Hangs up.

"Where do I go for a couple of hours?"

"Call your partner and suggest a drink. At Grimaldi's. Tell him we had an argument and you need to talk, but watch your tone. Anybody who sits in close proximity to you on a daily basis, as he does, will have thoughts."

"Tell me the story."

"It begins a year ago, when I got into a situation in Troy and you and Bobby picked me up and brought me in for questioning."

"Situation? You were destroying a pay phone with your bare hands."

"You remember when Bobby promised me if I ever needed anything, 'within so-called legal limits'? Because he knew who my father was and wanted to get on my good side? After I leave you two, I take the train home and sit opposite an abusive father who slapped his crying baby hard, less than a year old, black-and-blue marks from abusive episodes are visible. The wife, too, he's after."

The answering machine. Robinson: "I'll be over at eight sharp and I hope to Christ you can keep your famous rage in check."

"The famous rage he refers to was displayed on the train. On the body of the abusive father."

"How?"

"I pick him up off the seat by the throat. I'm choking him. He loses control of his bowels. He's about to leave the planet when I drop him back onto the seat. No more abuse. In Utica, they get off. I follow and take down his plate."

"Tell me you're making this up. What's this got to do with Bobby? You almost killed a man on the train? Tell me you're making this up. Have you ever done anything like that before—what you did on the train? Get to the part about Bobby's involvement."

"Bobby talks to his FBI contact and tells me the abuser, a man named Jed Kinter, has Mafia background as a hit man, who came to Utica one month before the famous triple hit here back in the nineties."

"The abuser turns out to be the hitter?"

"Yes."

"What's this have to do with Bobby?"

"Main target, one of the bosses of the Five Families who's in Utica for the funeral of his godmother. The other two killed were Freddy Barbone's Mafia father and uncle. My father wanted the Barbones dead because they were putting the squeeze on him for city contracts."

"That's public knowledge except for the identity of the hitter and my God! The role of your father. You keep leaving out the role of you and Bobby."

"We pick up the hitter, Bobby and I. We take him to a deserted place. Bobby and I. Antonio comes at my request. Antonio executes the hitter in our presence."

"My chief did murder? He did murder? You and Bobby are witnesses? Accomplices? Which is it? Witnesses or accomplices?"

"Yes."

"Yes what? Witnesses or accomplices? Why not just arrest him? This Mafia hitter?"

" 'The evidence,' Antonio says before he blows the hitter's brains out. Four in the head, Catherine. Four. A rage murder. 'The evidence is obvious to normal people,' Antonio says, 'but will not hold up in court.' Antonio makes the body disappear. None of this ever comes out."

"The Chief knew who Bobby was? His name? Where he came from?"

"Never laid eyes on him until that night. There were no introductions. Bobby was just an unknown face."

"Somehow he found out?"

"Yes, I think so."

"He arranged to hit Bobby? Eliminate a witness?"

"Yes. I think so. But it might as well have been me who arranged it. I brought Bobby in. I'm as responsible as Antonio."

"Why not you too? Why wouldn't he come for you too?"

"Antonio is not a monster."

"The hell he isn't."

"He won't come for me." (He's faking it well.) "But I worry he'll go for Bobby again, who can finger Antonio."

"And now that we're together?"

"He might assume that I've told you all."

"So you arrange to put me in witness protection in North Dakota?"

"I've got a problem."

"*We* have a problem, Eliot."

"Maybe Antonio had nothing to do with the attempt on Bobby's life. That's my hope, but this is what we need to nail down, one way or the other. You're staying here tonight."

(He picks up another piece of tomato pie. Puts it back.)

"The hell I am! You just told Antonio I'd be out."

"Stay. We'll talk in the living room. You hide quiet as a mouse behind the door in the spare room."

She's speechless.

"There's more to the story, but we don't have time. He'll be here in ten minutes. The conversation will interest you."

The phone. The answering machine: "My deepest apologies, Professor Conte. I am Novak Ivanovic, father of Mirko. Please come to our home. I beg you. Something terrible is happening. 608 Nichols Street. Directly across from Saint Stanislaus."

Eliot goes to the front window, squinting through the driving snow. Barely makes out Antonio's Mercedes as it pulls up.

She's already slipped into the spare room, closed the door, .38 in hand. Because she knew why he wanted her to stay. He didn't have to spell it out. Robinson sits for several endless minutes in the car, doing God knows what. Conte moves quickly to the master bedroom, behind the kitchen. Removes his loaded .357 Magnum from his bedside table. Moves quickly back to the living room, where he places it under a cushion on the couch. Then retreats to the kitchen.

As usual, he enters without knocking. Eliot comes to greet him, as Robinson, without removing it, shakes his snow encrusted, long black Italian overcoat the way a Labrador retriever shakes itself off emerging drenched from a cold pond in November, with a dead duck held softly in its mouth. For all their size and formidable deep voices, Labs are gentle, Eliot thinks, but maybe I'm Antonio's soon-to-be dead duck.

What I only deserve, he thinks, for what I made happen to Robert Rintrona.

They embrace.

Antonio says, "When I pull up I get a pain in the ass call from Homeland Security. You'll be interested. They seek a person of concern who's close to you."

Eliot speaks slowly and quietly:

"A beautiful coat like that, Chief, deserves a proper hanging." (Pause.) "As does its handsome owner."

"Fuck's that supposed to mean?"

CHAPTER 3

Still buttoned to the throat, collar turned up, Robinson sits at the desk that faces the big window giving onto the street—Mary Street disappearing in a blizzard. He turns the swivel chair around to face the couch, where Conte sits thinking that his best friend appears somehow profoundly relaxed and hyperalert and about to spring all at the same time.

"Fuckin' shivers all day, El." (He's lying.)

"Fever?"

Conte rises, approaches. Robinson stiffens. Palm on Robinson's forehead: "I'll get you a couple of aspirin."

Conte goes to the bathroom cabinet. Robinson quickly checks beneath his coat, left side, chest level. Rebuttons. His breathing shallow. Heart racing. Conte returns with two aspirin and a glass of water. Before he takes the aspirin, Robinson says, "Something smells good. Pizza?"

"No."

"Tomato pie?"

"Yes."

"Tell me O'Scugnizzo, El."

"Napoli's, Robby."

"Shit."

"Napoli's is good."

"Since when do you patronize, El?"

"Catherine."

(Pause.)

"Where's the foxy lady?"

"Out."

(Pause.)

"I haven't eaten supper, El." (He's lying.)

"I'll get you a couple of pieces."

"More than a couple, El."

When Conte goes to the kitchen, Robinson checks beneath the coat again. Conte returns with a plate of four pieces. As Robinson annihilates the first in under twenty seconds, Conte says, "Homeland Security?"

Robinson with a mouthful, "Mirko Ivanovic."

"Ridiculous."

"This new Imam at the new mosque on Mary and Albany? Can't pronounce his name—who can except these Arab types?"

"They're Bosnians."

"They're Muslims, El. This new Imam? He does online interaction with radical clerics in London and Yemen and this Mirko who you praise in my company? He's questionably in contact with the new Imam."

"Questionable how?"

"No idea. All I know, concerns are being explored concerning the interfaith gathering on Sunday."

"And?"

Robinson takes another huge bite.

"Put that fucking piece down for a minute."

"They won't give me details, arrogant federal cocksuckers,

no offense to your gay friends. They talked to the Imam a few hours ago. In custody, El. They seek your Mirko, who can't be located. I get this from the executive coordinator of Oneida County Homeland Security himself, Mark Martello, whose boyfriend or lover or whatever the word is—did they tie the knot yet? The boyfriend is—"

"My personal trainer, Kyle. So what?"

"He'll be calling you in the morning for background on Mirko. Martello says he has deep concern. He said deep more than once. They have a working theory about the interfaith gathering on Sunday afternoon which includes Utica's toughest Jews. Martello tells me your name is on the guest list." (How could it be? He'd accepted the invitation only late this afternoon, and he was on a list already accessed by Homeland Security?) "Martello tells me the mayor is on the list. My theory is Martello theorizes a bomb on Sunday afternoon. Al Qaeda. We have something international in our midst, El, and your boy—"

"You channel anti-Muslim crap? Since when?"

"I'm you, El, I don't show on Sunday afternoon. Our asshole mayor, on the other hand—"

"I know Mark Martello. The four of us have dinner occasionally. He's normal, reasonable, with an understated sense of humor. Not paranoid."

"All well and good. His homosexuality is not a factor here."

"Who said it was?"

"El, live and fuckin' let live is my philosophy. But keep in mind, however so-called normal this three-dollar bill Martello is, the sophisticated monitoring goes on way above Marky boy's pretty head. They pick up the chatter of the jihadists. Via Montana, D.C., Langley, via outer fuckin' space, wherever they have surveillance devices of enormous power they look right up our—my guess? They think you might be closely guarding information as to the whereabouts of Mirko Ivanovic, if they're not thinking you're harboring the little raghead. They likely don't rule out criminal complicity on your part, El. In my opinion."

"Don't make me laugh."

"Are you?"

"Am I what?"

"Complicitous?"

"You're working hard, Antonio, to divert from the real subject we're here to discuss."

"All these years you call me Robby—now it's Antonio?"

"So what?"

"What do I know, El? This is my speculation. Martello is cagy. Homosexuals, in my extremely limited experience, can be very indirect about what's really on their secret minds."

"How much of this are you making up? Because you're beginning to piss me off."

"You teach fiction, I deal in harsh facts on a daily basis"—as he takes another piece. Eats. Requests a napkin. Conte goes to the kitchen. Robinson glances quick and hard at the closed door to the spare room. Touches his upper-left chest.

Conte returns with an elegant cloth napkin: "When I feel what you're feeling now, I do what you're doing."

"What's that, Professor?"

"Don't play dumb. We binge eat when we have fear and anxiety. We eat and we divert and we avoid. Today we're binge-eating brothers. I don't believe you missed your supper tonight. Al Qaeda in Afghanistan, Al Qaeda in Iraq, Al Qaeda in East Africa, Al Qaeda in Yemen. And now you come here with a story. Al Qaeda in Utica, New York. Al Qaeda in a small, sad, economically destroyed town fading fast into the sub-cellar of American history. Utica, New York, the looming site of a major terrorist attack. Utica, New York, displaces Manhattan, D.C., Boston, Chicago, and L.A. as the focus of Al Qaeda's desire to do mass murder to America's innocent civilians. All GPS devices manufactured from here on out position and measure distances from the new global center: Utica, New York. Where the fuck is Islamabad? Nine thousand miles east southeast of Utica, New York. And my gentle student, whose goal is to teach literature in high school, is a key operative of terror."

"Hey! El! Don't think I didn't voice skepticism along your lines, which is why I sat out there so long shivering in the car, talking to Mark Martello. Know what he said? He says, Chief, all due respect. The handful of big cities can be defended, maybe, but small town America has no chance. The people in small towns, he says, they think they're beyond the reach and they're secretly wishing the worst for the big cities of the immoral liberal elites. Martello says they believe—the small town types, the rural types—that on 9/11 New York got what it fuckin' deserved and too bad all of Wall Street wasn't destroyed, where they steal our money on a daily basis. Fuck the elites. Fuck Manhattan. This is what the real America thinks, Martello says. Now real America is about to take it hard up the ass, though because of his erotic persuasion Mark doesn't quite put it that way. You forget, El, that

Muhammad Atta was a gentle-appearing little guy, a possible faggot, just like your Mirko? An intellectual, just like your little Mirko?"

"You've taken care of four pieces in no time and you want more, don't you?"

"I do, El."

"What happened in Troy this morning—this is the source of your binge."

Robinson points to the closed door of the spare room: "I've been coming here weekly since you moved back, twenty years ago. Know what I notice tonight that I never once saw in twenty years? I notice that that son of a bitchin' door, which has never been closed when I visit, is closed for the first time in twenty years. This is my fuckin' observation."

"Forget the spare room."

"Mirko Ivanovic in there?"

"Anything is possible."

"Catherine?"

"Anything is possible."

Robinson undoes the top two buttons of his coat. Conte's right hand slips between the cushion he's sitting on and the cushion beneath which he's hidden his .357 Magnum.

Conte says, "It's possible that the real Osama bin Laden is hiding in there, his double having been killed, and it's possible that you and I will do something foolish. You with what you're packing under your coat and I with what I have under here, with the safe off—the safe is off, Robby, and I can get it out well before you get yours. I advise you to take your coat off. Carefully. Now."

Robinson complies, revealing what Conte had suspected

was there from the beginning. Conte says, "Good," and pulls out the .357 Magnum. Lays it on the cushion. Conte says, "Is the fear which we have for one another tonight well grounded? That's the only question."

Conte stands. He says, "I'm going to the kitchen to bring out the entire box from Napoli's, so that we can both feed our anxiety. I'll leave my revolver there on the couch while I go to the kitchen. I'll be turning my back on you. Either we are who we've been for each other for fifty years or we're done. I'm gone and your life is worthless and you'll eat your gun sooner or later with your brains on the wall." In the spare room, .38 at the ready, Catherine Cruz peers in vain between the door's edge and the doorjamb. Conte turns his back.

He returns with the box and lays it on the coffee table fronting the couch. Neither will eat. Neither, tonight, will die. Conte ejects the rounds from his .357. Robinson follows suit. The woman in the spare room will feel soon the death of whatever innocence about love she's retained at age forty-one.

"You want to know how I knew that the man shot in Troy this morning is your pal, as I said on the phone?"

"Yes."

"Because the sexy Detective Cruz casually mentioned you two go down there to have dinner with her ex-partner, whose name we already had when Catherine transferred up here. Obviously. Which proves nothing about my guilt or innocence. Obviously."

"Obviously."

"If I'm playing a game, El, I don't tell you, as I tell you

now, that I knew about Rintrona and your connection with him for a year—ever since that Saturday we went down to Troy for *Carmen* in hi def, the day you told me your kids on the West Coast had just been murdered. You disappear after the first intermission. I see you back here that night, looking like a wild man, and you tell me you destroyed a telephone booth in Troy in your impotent fuckin' rage for your children's death, not to mention the ton of guilt for leaving them as babies thirty years ago. You told me you were arrested for the phone booth. Naturally, curious officer of the law that I am, I check out the arrest data with my opposite number in Troy and your name, Catherine's, and Rintrona's show up. Tell me something, you motherfucker, do I sound like I'm trying to hide something? Several days later in the dark I do what I do, which you wanted done, you summoned me there, let's not bullshit ourselves, you wanted him dead, El, in the company of a third party I never saw before, his face is not that clear in that dark wasteland, but clear enough. Because when I check out the Troy Police website that night on a hunch, bingo! I recognize him. Robert Rintrona. Okay? I've known he was a witness for more than a year. And someone else knew about Troy—my ex-assistant chief who reviewed police logs from around the state. He told me with pleasure what I already knew—that the spoiled son of Silvio Conte, so forth and so on. Fuck him and the horse he rode in on. I'm telling you all of it up front and you think I'm behind the attempt on his life? I wait a whole fuckin' year to eliminate a threat of that magnitude? Use your fuckin' head, Professor. Use your fuckin' head because you're so smart."

"You came here armed."

"Because I know the levels of rage you can go to. What you did on the train."

"You blew that bastard away, Antonio."

"Which you wanted. Stop bullshitting yourself. He was abusive to his child on the train, which is how you see yourself in a fucked-up way, as an abusive father. You abandon your babies, when they're two and three, and eventually they die because you're not there. I kill the animal you see as your double and you don't have to kill yourself."

Conte feels the urge to leap over the table and strangle. He fires a piece of tomato pie off Robinson's chest.

Robinson does not react.

"You played a key role in my father's plot. You helped engineer a triple murder."

"Did you just say the words 'my father'? He took me in when I was eight without a father. I just about lived with you and Silvio. He loved me. You know he did."

(Pause.)

"He did. Silvio loved you, Robby. Maybe more than me."

"And I agreed to help him take down all that Mafia scum because he gave me life. Where were you? When we did it? When I did the right thing because the Barbones were about to destroy our father? Where the fuck were you, the beloved biological son?"

(With averted eyes:)

"In Austria. Taking in the Salzburg Festival."

"You fuckin' opera queen."

"You're not one too?"

(They almost smile.)

"Austria, on your father's money. All that boring Mozart.

Who bought this house for you when you abandoned the West Coast, broke? Daddy. Who remodels it? Daddy. The son who gives him such a hard time, but thanks to Daddy you live in a small jewel, the only bungalow on Mary Street. Now with the inheritance you're free to pursue your literary proclivities. The White Whale. The Scarlet Cunt. That faggot in disguise, Homo Hemingway. I did murder so you could be spared our bloody life, is how Silvio and I thought of it. So you could be spared for literature. Literature. The word makes me puke. You think I was behind the attempt on Rintrona today?"

Conte pauses.

"Not really."

"What does 'not really' mean? What do you mean by 'really'? That the jury in your head is still out?"

"No. The jury is not out."

"Why not?"

Conte pauses.

"You never killed anybody. Until that night. For once in your life—for once you went against yourself to do violence—on behalf of our father. Our father."

"El, this is getting too hard for me."

"If not you, Robbie—"

"If?"

"You know what I mean."

"Do I, El?"

At the door, Robinson says, "Everything I told you about Homeland Security?"

"Total bullshit, I gather?"

"Every word—totally true."

"Including your speculations?"

"Don't go to the mosque on Sunday, El. Uh, El, may I take a slice of the tomato pie with me?"

Conte nods with a small smile. Robinson leaves. Conte collapses on the couch. An ashen Catherine Cruz emerges from the spare room. She stands before him in cold fury:

"Eliot. Do you know who I am? Don't respond. I'll tell you when you may. I am an officer of the law who you just made a witness to my chief's confession to several murders. You were an active accomplice. You summoned Antonio Robinson to do murder. Now I either go to the D.A. or I swim in this sewer with you. You wanted me here to hear it all. Why? Do not respond. I'm not finished. Not because you believed you needed an armed guard in case Antonio went off the deep end. The gentlest man you've ever known, you always say. Who nevertheless did murder. A pussy, you said. Who did murder. He's sweet, we both said. For what possible reason did you want me here? To make me an accessory after the fact? I'm finished."

Conte rises to embrace her. She backs away. She says, "Answer me."

(Very long pause.)

"So you could know exactly who you were living with."

She says nothing.

"Are you leaving me, Catherine?"

She says nothing.

"Catherine. Have you stopped loving me?"

Looking the saddest he's ever seen her look, she says, "How could I ever do that?"

"Will you go to the D.A.? I think you have to."

"How could I ever do that? Explain to me, Eliot, how I could ever do that."

He moves to her. She steps back.

"I owe you the truth, Catherine. Antonio was wrong about my motive for bringing the hit man to his execution."

"You mean Antonio's hot air that you needed to have the abusive father–hit man killed because he was your so-called double? You deliver him to his death and somehow lose your guilt for leaving your babies?"

"Yes. Bullshit."

"But in your mind your kids would be alive today if only—"

"Yes."

"We both failed our kids, Eliot. You'll never escape the thought that if you only had stayed."

"You write big checks for Miranda."

"I do."

"Guilt checks?"

"Of course, Eliot."

"It helps?"

"Of course not."

"Nothing to be done, Catherine?"

"Try to live now."

"Are we?"

"Barely. Barely. I'm committed to you no matter what you did. Level with me."

"I did it for Antonio."

"Who meant more to you than even your own father."

"The hitter knew of Antonio's role in the triple hit."

"Which is why you wanted him dead."

"Yes."

"Loyalty to Antonio trumped thou shalt not kill."

"Yes."

"Loyalty trumps everything? Your only moral principle?"

"Definitely."

"You have a Mafia mentality, Eliot."

"You just told me, didn't you, you wouldn't go to the D.A. in spite of what you know? You, an officer of the law, no less."

"Want me to say I also have a Mafia mentality?"

"I want you to say we're in this together."

"Eliot, we're in the pitch dark together."

CHAPTER 4

Face to face, still, in the front room.

Conte moves to embrace her. She again backs away.

He says, "Where are we, really?"

No response.

"I need to talk with Mirko's father."

No response.

"I need to go now."

She turns her back—walks to the window—stares out at the storm. By morning, no vehicles will move for three days, the employees of the supermarkets will stay home, and the few remaining Mom-and-Pop corner grocery stores will do booming business for the first time in a long time, and likely for the last.

He leaves in a heavy leather jacket and scarf. No hat. (Conte never wears a hat.) Steps west on Mary, destination 608 Nichols Street—glancing down his driveway with some relief. Good. He'd parked behind her. No way out unless she walks or takes a cab. Where could she possibly go, anyway, whose only social companions were also his? Kyle Torvald and Mark Martello, every two or three weeks for dinner. Antonio and Millicent Robinson, just once in the six months since she'd moved to Utica, as Robinson and Eliot drifted apart.

Huddled into himself—eyes downcast and shoulders hunched up against the wind and cold—walking west, always west on Mary, he reaches Bacon, first of the three cross streets he must cross—then Milgate, then Jefferson—dropped deep inside himself now as the surging music in his head almost perfectly obliterates matters of murder—it was glorious, the concert in Berlin he and Catherine and Bobby and Maureen Rintrona had taken in, in Troy, in high-definition telecast, a month ago—all that vocal opulence again flooding Conte's head as he passes the Nichols cross street where he must turn right toward Bleecker—thinking of the gift he'll spring on her—first-class airline tickets and choice seats at the Royal Opera House in Stockholm, where the concert will be reprised. Would she go now? Will she leave him now? She said she wouldn't, but if she should leave? She said she ... but if she does? What then? What does he do about it? The same thing he did about his children's murders. Nothing. On his gravestone: *Eliot the Impotent. Herein lies a man who could not act when it truly mattered.*

Lost in the narrow space of himself and long past Nichols when the illuminated tower of Saint Agnes breaks through his reverie and snaps him back into the physical world—bootless shoes in seven inches of heavy, wet snow—hatless head and shoulders wearing a thick white cape—Conte backtracking quickly now toward Nichols when a darkened figure of substantial size comes running hard straight at him. Conte gives no ground. The man abruptly swerves, almost falling, into the front yard of an ill-maintained two-family house. The man drops his pants. The man squats. The man commences to defecate massively—pants down at his ankles still—squatting still—grunting and moaning and shitting. Conte roars "not in my neighborhood." And in a sudden burst he's upon him and flipping him over and mashing the man's face into the steaming heap with his knees ground into the man's upper back—220 pounds of Conte—Conte whispering, "In my neighborhood?" The man inhaling shit and snow. The man suffocating. Conte rises. The man gagging, coughing, vomiting. Without daring to look up at his assailant, the man says, "Why?" Conte whispers, "This is East Utica." Pulls off the man's pants, walks to the sewer at the corner of Mary and Nichols, stuffs them in. The bare-assed man races off bare-assed into the night.

Two more minutes to the Ivanovic house. He's on his way—having acted when it truly did not matter.

608 Nichols: imitation Victorian elegance, common on the East Side of town. Narrow across the front, very deep and high, with a full-windowed attic lending it the aspect of a stately three-storey structure. (Worth about thirty-five grand in a buyer's market.) Recently painted dead white, Conte sees it shimmer through the screen of the wind-slanted snow like a haunted house in a grade-B Hollywood horror film. All windows are dark except one on the first floor, where Novak Ivanovic has been standing for an hour—peering intently out from behind barely parted heavy drapes, awaiting Conte's arrival. What he sees ascending the steps, into the pool of uncertain light cast by the flickering porch fixture, is a big man with a reassuring demeanor. (Ivanovic needs reassurance.) The big man slicks off the snow from his head. This big man, thinks

Ivanovic, this very picture of professorial composure, who presses the nonfunctional doorbell—this must be Eliot Conte.

They sit in the parlor, as it is called in East Utica, on chairs of hostile design—no arms, ass-bruising seats. Ivanovic has convinced a reluctant Conte to remove his drenched shoes and socks and to accept a pair of his heavy woolens. Conte's shoes amaze Ivanovic. (Ivanovic knows shoes.) Never has he seen anything like them in Utica or Syracuse stores. He's curious where they can be found, but suppresses the urge to ask and feels deeply ashamed to have let such thoughts into his mind in the context of his family crisis. (Beautiful, these Bruno Magli shoes.) Conte accepts a towel for his soaked head. Ivanovic will speak when he's finished toweling off. Conte drops the towel to the floor. Ivanovic opens his mouth, but nothing comes out.

"Talk to me, Mr. Ivanovic."

"Professor Conte—"

"Call me Eliot."

"Thank you. I am Novak. Please help me. Please."

(Silence: mutual discomfort rising.)

"Talk to me. Where's Mirko?"

"I don't know."

"Your wife knows, Novak."

"She doesn't."

"She's lying." (Civilized professor gives way quickly to the rough-edged former private investigator, lurking beneath.)

"How can you say this of my wife that she is lying?"

"Used to be my business."

"Lying wives?"

"Missing kids. Boys. They confide in the mothers. The

father as usual's in the dark. Yeah, lying wives too who do extramarital f–, screwing."

"They came this afternoon, Eliot."

"Mark Martello."

"Yes."

"Who else?"

"Only him."

"You said 'they,' Novak."

"Forgive me. With a thing like this I feel again the force of the government in my home country. There, it is never one. Always many. Forgive me. Only Mr. Martello."

"Who said what, exactly?"

"That my Mirko may have entered into questionable contact with our new Imam. Questionable contact, he said. Was he at home? No, I said. Do you know where he is? No, I said. Mr. Martello said if I knew and did not tell that I myself would become questionable."

"Did you lie to Martello?"

"No."

"Are you lying to me now?"

"No."

"I'm reserving judgment, Novak."

"Please, Eliot."

"Did he ask to speak to your wife?"

"Yes. I told him she was quite sick and could not be disturbed."

"Is she sick? Were you lying to Martello?"

"In a way, she is always sick, in a way. Eliot, I fear Homeland Security."

"We all do."

"What can I do?"

"Nothing."

"Sit in my home and become crazy?"

"Yes."

"Can you help me?"

"I'll talk to Martello tomorrow."

"Tell him Mirko is good."

"That's not the point, Novak."

"That is the only point, Eliot."

(Pause.)

"I need to talk to your wife. Tonight."

Ivanovic leads Conte into the dining room—a table of sumptuous African Rosewood and chairs with merciful seats, in contrast to the flesh-denying Danish furniture in the parlor. Two places set with expensive china and silverware and two serving dishes loaded with pastry. Ivanovic pours the coffee. Though an insatiable pastry hound from childhood, Conte cannot help asking why so much. Ivanovic says, "This is from The Florentine and this from Caruso's. It is impossible to eat all of these. I know this. Not wise for my cholesterol, but I cannot go to The Florentine without going to Caruso's. If I go only to The Florentine and Ricky Caruso sees me with the bag, it causes me to believe that I am causing Ricky to feel sad. This thought causes me to feel sad. Now, neither Ricky or I feel sad."

"You're a good man, Novak. Now take me to your wife."

"Not a good idea."

"Who are the upstairs tenants?"

"We are."

"The three of you on two floors?"

"Unfortunately."

"Who lives on the second floor?"

"My wife and Mirko."

"The attic? Anybody up there?"

"No."

"When *they* come back, *they* will go through this place with a fine-tooth comb."

"You may talk to my wife, but she will not talk to you. Since the separation, she went up there and I stayed down here and she will not speak."

Neither has yet touched the pastries or the coffee. Neither will.

"When she hears me ascending the stairs, she locks the door, unless it is time for me to bring dinner. My wife gets no exercise, Eliot. She is filling out, as they say."

"Take me to Mirko's room."

"He's not there."

"I need to look at the room. Now."

They ascend the darkened stairs—the door to the wife's room is closed. Sounds of a radio tuned to a rap station. The door to Mirko's room is open.

"Your wife or Mirko in the attic? Which one?"

"Mirko is gone. I do not lie."

Conte goes to the desk in Mirko's room, picks up the laptop, "For the sake of Mirko and your family I'm taking this before *they* do." Conte notes the large poster of Natalie Portman in *Black Swan*. Grace and pain. A jihadist's icon? He says, "I'm going to look through the drawers of the desk and bureau." (Ivanovic believes that all is hopeless now. His family will be destroyed.) Nothing of interest until beneath a stack of T-shirts he finds a photo of a girl, twenty or so, dark haired, Hispanic, drop-dead beautiful. On the back: "Love, Delores." Conte's first theory of the case flashes to mind. Muslim boy and Catholic girl run off from disapproving parents. A cliché, but then most stories are. Checks the closet. Asks Ivanovic if Mirko has a suitcase. They each have only one. Up to the attic to check the number of suitcases. There are three.

Ivanovic offers to drive Conte home. Conte refuses, requesting only that he be given a sturdy shopping bag in which to carry the unprotected computer. Ivanovic suggests he keep the warm woolen socks. Conte refuses and replaces them with his own, still wet. At the door, Ivanovic says, "You must answer a question before you leave. When I said that Mirko was good, you replied, That's not the point. Tell me now, Professor, what, if not that, is the point?"

Conte opens the door, steps out into the flickering light, turns and says, "I have no idea."

On the path up to his front door, he checks for footprints in the deepening snow. There's his, almost covered up. Another set, fresher, leading from the front door to the curb and ending there. She's gone. Cab? Belmonte? Kyle? Calls Kyle who tells him he hasn't heard, but would like to. Ditto Don Belmonte. Calls both of Utica's dying cab companies and is told they don't give out such information except to the police. When he tells the dispatchers that he's a P.I., one immediately hangs up, the other hangs up too but not before saying, "Get real, asshole." Thoughts of Johnnie Walker when the phone rings. Caller I.D.: Antonio Robinson.

"Yeah, Robby."

"You crazy fuck."

"Thanks, Robby."

"Are you all there, El? Are you fuckin' all there? You sick fuck. Listen to me. A poor son of a bitch on Mary in the vicinity of Nichols suddenly experiences terrific intestinal cramps that lead in one direction only and fuckin' *imminently*! He starts to run, which only makes the situation worse. He's hoping to get home in time. Tragically, he fails. Then something happens, after which the poor guy runs down Mary with his coat around his middle and his face—I don't want to get into the face. At a certain point near Kossuth, he darts into an alley where he collapses in humiliation and tries to wash off his face with snow. Thank God, El, thank God he put his cell in his coat pocket and not his pants. He calls his wife et cetera. Here's where things get ticklish. The investigating detective is so stunned by the story that he calls me at home about the event. Which my wife doesn't appreciate. He rough describes the assailant. Not that he had to because as soon as the detective tells me what was done to him, I conclude there's only one man in this hemisphere who's capable of this unusual act of insanity. What do you have to say, El, before I say more?"

"Nothing."

"You know you did this, don't you, El?"

"I guess."

"You guess? You *guess*?"

Conte doesn't respond.

"A twelve-step program for rageaholics. There are such things. Because you need attention. You need to find a cure, man, before you kill somebody. You don't want to do that."

"Okay."

"Okay what?"

"I believe you that I don't want to kill somebody. You should know, better than me."

"Don't get snotty."

"Didn't mean to be, Robby."

"You snotty cunt."

"Sorry."

"When's the last time the two of us had lunch, just the two of us, never mind the women?"

"Who knows."

"You crazy fuck."

He hangs up. Calls Hotel Utica. No one registered under the name of Catherine Cruz.

Without hat or gloves or scarf, without jacket, he steps back out into the cold that's gotten colder and the wind heavier and the snow driven harder, in hopeless search of the anonymous man he's humiliated in order to—to what? He cannot say. To ask forgiveness for his appalling behavior? (*Yes.*) To say to a man he'll never find, "Forgive me, I myself am appalling"? (*Better.*) "Be so kind as to absolve me of myself." (*Best of all.*)

Down Mary he goes again in the vicinity of Nichols, then farther west to Saint Agnes, Utica's church of the virgin who was martyred for her faith at thirteen. His search, like her shattering martyrdom, to no avail. Home again now on this deserted street of frail, wind-blasted houses. Mounting the front steps now at 1318 Mary, not shivering. Bone-numbing cold is his element. Inside, he's careful to avoid reflections of himself in windows and mirrors.

Most grievous transgression of all, says a voice in his head, *your abandoned babies.*

Conte checking listings of hotels and motels in Utica and its immediate environs. Call them all? Stares long at the phone, but cannot reach for the receiver. Five-hundred-pound boulders attached to his wrists. Head down on desk, drifting off toward oblivion on the Good Ship Depression, as he broods on Angel Moreno, the thirteen-year-old boy next door, who told Eliot, weeks before it was announced ... Angel guaranteed it ... The Yankees would trade Jesus Montero for Michael Pineda of the Seattle Mariners ... "It's happening, Jefe ... Brian like told me ..." "Brian?..." "The GM, Jefe ... Brian, he cc'd me on the plan ... Brian like copies me daily, man ..."

CHAPTER 5

Forty-five minutes later Conte's pulled up from dreamless sleep by the phone:

"Catherine."

"Yes."

"You."

"Yes."

"Where—?"

"Best Western."

"North Utica?"

"There is no other."

"When will you—?"

"Maybe never."

"But you said—"

"I called Antonio, Eliot."

(Silence.)

"Told him I'm taking a leave of absence."

(Silence.)

"Starting tomorrow."

(Silence.)

"I'm considering resigning. Strongly considering."

(Silence.)

"Contemplating a return to Troy."

(Silence.)

"Catherine."

(Silence.)

"Are you still there, Catherine?"

"Yes."

"When will I see you?"

"Tomorrow. I need to collect my things."

(Silence.)

"Goodnight, Eliot."

"Wait—"

The line goes dead. Head back down on desk until 3 A.M. when he awakes and walks stiffly, bent over, to the bedroom of the empty bed—pulling off the down comforter—dragging it back to the front room like a three-year-old dragging his special blanket, where he covers himself on the couch in fitful sleep until morning.

Angel Moreno. Cc'd daily by the general manager of the New York Yankees? By Brian Cashman himself? Four A.M., tossing and turning, hatching a theory—and a plan.

At 8 he awakens to an excited young voice in mounting volume—a boy on the street—just outside Conte's front picture window—kicking a soccer ball in the unplowed snow while announcing in speed-of-light Spanish an assault on goal. GOOOOOOOOOAL! In yesterday's clothes, with yesterday's breath, hair spiked out in several directions: Conte opens the front door and calls him over, Angel Moreno.

"Hey! Hey! What d'ya say a cup of hot chocolate topped with whipped cream? How about it?"

"Jefe! You like in a dangerous mood?"

"Up all night, Angel, grading papers."

"Grading make you crazy? You look wild, man!"

"Hot chocolate, Angel?"

"You drink that shit, Jefe?"

"Cappuccino for me."

"The chocolate thing, man, it's for babies and like old people in end-of-life situations. Offer me a cappuccino, Jefe, because I feel Italian this morning."

"What would your good parents say?"

"I don't feature speculation, Jefe."

"You really want a cappuccino?"

"Can you spare one?"

At the threshold: The man, 6'3", 220. The boy, 5'5½", 97 pounds. The big man is in over his head.

Utica in paralysis: a no-school day, a no-bus-service day, a no-traffic day except for city plows working against a twenty-three-inch fall of heavy snow. At the kitchen table, Angel raising his cup in a toast and saying, "Jefe, you be the man."

"Angel, we've talked about this before. You *are* the man is correct."

"You *be* the man, Professor. Angel has his reasons."

"Tell me why you insist on calling me Jefe."

"Because you be the *boss*, the *leader*. You be *El Jefe*. Because what is the infinitive form under scrutiny? *To be*. You *are* has like no balls. Whereas *El Jefe* in his self is like unconjugated, man."

"Tell me something, Angel."

"Yeah."

"Where did you learn to talk like that? At thirteen?"

"The Net, Jefe. YouTube. Et cetera. Not to mention my Norwegian colleagues."

"Angel, let's review your personal history. When you were seven. Then I want to propose something secret between us."

"Jefe, I have to say something powerful."

"What's that?"

"I don't feature pedophilia."

"I didn't hear that, Angel."

"Just sayin'."

"You stole a bottle of expensive perfume, when you were seven. You were nailed in the act. Your good parents were humiliated."

"It was a Christmas present for my mother, Jefe, and as a seven year old I didn't have the money. Like why would a seven year old have the money? Like why should a fuckin' little child have to pay for a present for his mother? Where's the morality in that, Jefe?"

"They grounded you for a year."

"Yeah."

"They came to me for advice."

"El Jefe, yeah."

"I advised that you'd go crazy if you didn't have something to do all those weekends."

"Yeah."

"So they bought you a computer six years ago."

"No, Jefe. *You* bought it. They couldn't afford."

"You're not supposed to know that."

"Yeah."

"They didn't tell me you made yourself a wizard."

"They don't know the half of it."

"I think I do."

"Yeah?"

"You made yourself a radical hacker. A hacktivist."

"Don't flatter the truth, Jefe."

"Brian Cashman cc's you daily because you hack into his e-mail?"

"Yeah."

"Wow."

"Some of my Norwegian colleagues, they like have their sights on the fuckin' CIA, Jefe, but not me."

"You draw the line at the CIA?"

"I'm going for Barack's BlackBerry."

"You do know his BlackBerry was specially made with encryption beyond hacking?"

"Jefe?"

"Yes?"

"Don't make me laugh."

"Even if you succeed, they trace it back to you."

"No problem, señor."

"Why not?"

"I'm thirteen, señor."

"I've got tomato pie. Hungry?"

"O'Scugnizzo's or Napoli's?"

"Napoli's."

"Forget it, man."

"Would you like to earn two hundred dollars, Angel?"

"Like I said, Jefe, I don't feature pedo—"

"Hold your tongue!"

"Hold my *tongue*? What's that, man? Some new perversion maneuver?"

Conte leaves the kitchen and returns with a computer: "How long would it take you to hack into the e-mail?"

"Two hours."

"Two hundred dollars?"

"Cool."

"What if I could give you the owner's name?"

"One hour."

"Cash, Angel, two hundred."

"You be requesting an illegal act, Jefe."

"Three hundred."

"Yeah."

"Mirko Ivanovic."

"Say what?"

"The owner's name."

"I don't have no hard feelings for no Bosnians."

"Four hundred."

"Yeah. By the way, Jefe, you look unkept."

"You mean *unkempt*, Angel."

"Angel knows what he means: for sure you be *unkempt*, totally, without sayin'. But you also be *unkept*. She gone?"

"Out of curiosity, amigo—"

"Don't sweat it, Jefe."

"Do you talk this way to your parents?"

"Get serious, Jefe."

"To friends at school?"

"Jefe?"

"Talk to me, amigo."

"Angel don't feature friendship."

"Just me?"

"Plus my Norwegian associates. Jefe?"

"Yes."

"You look bad, man."

The phone. The answering machine. 8:45: "Eliot, Mark. We need to chat very soon about a matter of security. I'll be by at 10:30. It's worth your while to be there, if at all possible. Strictly unofficial, at this point."

Angel, feet up on kitchen table: "Would that be Mark Martello of the regional office?"

"It would."

"Heavy."

"I need to get showered and changed, and you need to work on that computer. It stays here. The computer doesn't leave."

"No problem, señor."

As Eliot leaves the room, Angel says, "Four bills is too totally generous. Angel hacks Martello's ass for you while he's at it, free of charge."

Eliot turns and says, with a grin, "Yeah."

"One more thing, Jefe. I'm sayin' don't come out of that shower naked and hard."

Thirty minutes later, Conte appears in the front room freshly dressed, shaved and showered, to find his friend lounging on the couch with a second cup of cappuccino, watching the Nature Channel's show on the primitive wolf.

"Don't have something better to do, Angel?"

"Than gaze on my father?" (Pointing to television.)

"You have a job. It's urgent."

"Formerly."

"Formerly?"

"It's all good."

"Speak normal English, Angel."

"Nineteen minutes and thirty-seven seconds. Candy from a baby, Jefe. The Bosnian machine is open for you over there to what you need. As far as Martello, he's interested in the Bosnian, but doesn't have squat. He's obsessing about this new Imam I can't pronounce his name at the new Muslim synagogue. The word Sunday is big. A major act on Sunday is my belief. This Mirko you can read yourself. Shall we discuss the payoff, Jefe?"

"I can have it for you no later than tomorrow, when I presume I'll be able to get out of the driveway and to the bank."

"I'll take one hundred in twenties then twenty per week for fifteen weeks."

"I'm happy to give it to you all at once."

"Can't asept four hundred cold."

"Why not?"

"You suffering memory dementia, Jefe? I'm *thirteen*, man."

Eliot asks what he'll do with his day off from school and Angel replies, "Barack's BlackBerry, while I dream of The Land of the Midnight Sun."

"You have quite a thing for Norway, Angel."

"Vice versa, Jefe."

Angel's out the door when it occurs to Conte: How did he manage to make a second cappuccino while he was in the shower? He calls out: "How did you know how to work the cappuccino machine?"

"A new associate of mine, Jefe. In Palermo."

Conte searches Mirko's sent file back several weeks—nothing to the Imam. Inbox dominated by messages from Delores Delgado, who he believes must be the beauty of the hidden photo. Obstacles to young lovers. Two different worlds. Mirko's reference to *Romeo and Juliet*. Delores's puzzlement. Mirko explaining Shakespeare by reference to *West Side Story*. Muslim boy, Catholic girl. Star-crossed. She didn't want him to use the word *tragic*, although she could be persuaded. There was a time and a place for them. Hold my hand. She said, "Please." A long trail of messages. Love makes the world go away. She said, "I'll take you there." Conte is convinced that Mirko and Delores have eloped. As of late yesterday afternoon, no longer in Utica. Mirko and terrorism? Joke. Angel was right. They don't have squat on Mirko. Conte suffers a pang of doubt. But who is this new Imam? Who, really, is Mirko Ivanovic outside the classroom?

Forty-five minutes to kill before Mark Martello arrives and Conte doesn't know what to do with himself. No appetite for breakfast—the call from Catherine—how cold she was.

Catherine maybe lost, who said she'd never leave him. He paces. Stops at the front window to stare out at Mary and Wetmore—Wetmore ascending from Utica's lowest point at Broad—crossing Catherine, crossing Bleecker—rising always to Mary, to end T-stopping directly before his house, 1318 Mary.

There again on the street—soccer ball replaced by a beat-up sled. Angel standing at the T-stop, looking down Wetmore—Conte looking at Angel looking down Wetmore. Should he warn him off the temptation? Wetmore zooming down to Bleecker, as the Lo Bianco boy zoomed down, who had not been warned, decades ago. His father told the story. Did Angel's parents know the story? Had the Italians of Mary Street passed on the story to the newcomers of Mary Street? Fear for your children on the hills of lower East Utica. The Lo Bianco boy, 1941, had not been feared for—zooming down Wetmore fearlessly—braking hard at Bleecker, where he hits a patch of wet leaves on a brilliant day in autumn and skids through the wet leaves hard and fast onto dry sidewalk and the bike flips and little Lo Bianco flies over the handle bars onto Bleecker on his belly as an eastbound bus rolls slowing toward the corner of Bleecker and Wetmore—rolling fatally to a stop—exactly onto the Lo Bianco boy's exploding head.

Angel turns from the temptation of Wetmore and sleds west along Mary. Out of sight. Where? To Mary and Bacon? Yet another temptation, as are all parallel north-south cross streets that rise to Mary and beyond and keep on rising until lower East Utica becomes upper East Utica. A rise once signifying elevation of real estate values—not, as now, elevated risks of arson, assault, drugs—as the relentless Anthony V. Senzalma never tires of reporting twice daily on syndicated talk radio.

Conte stashes Mirko's computer behind a bookshelf.

The silence of snowbound Mary is broken by the house-shaking rumbling roar of a military Humvee that stops at 1318. From the passenger's side, a tall, wiry, dashing man emerges, dressed in a pin-striped suit without overcoat, hat, or boots. An expensive Tuscan shoulder bag. Reaches into the Humvee.

Emerges with a brown bag. The Humvee will wait, throbbing at the curb. The dashing man enters with his offering:

"From my Italophilic companion. Lunch."

"Hello, Mark."

"El."

"Coffee?"

"No."

"This need refrigeration?"

"Sausage and peppers, El. Significant sandwiches for significant eaters."

"So this is only about friends on a lunch date?"

"Let's hope so, El."

"Ten thirty is early for sandwiches of this heft."

"Let's sit in the kitchen, El, where we have easy access to Kyle's kindness. Or have you lost your legendary appetite since Catherine walked?"

"How do you—"

"Accommodations at Best Western are gracious. Complimentary breakfast. Walking distance to Del Monico's Steak House. Kyle and I will try to talk her out of returning to Troy."

"So you've somehow tracked her—"

"Of course."

"Bastard."

"We leave no stone unturned."

"Bastard."

"I need your assistance, El. We have time. Not like tomorrow's Sunday."

"Today is Tuesday, Mark, and I'm about to tell you that you need to leave because unless you wish to officially detain—"

"Whoa! Big guy! This is about a friend helping a friend who may be dealing with a situation."

"Your concern originates from D.C.?"

"No comment."

"Janet Napolitano sending her squad of superpatriots?"

"No comment."

"Totally your initiative?"

"Yes. I don't intend to get burned."

"Your job that boring? Terrorism in Utica? Come on."

"Yep, boring. We have the sudden departure of Catherine Cruz. We have you visiting 608 Nichols Street last night, where Novak Ivanovic gave you something, which you carried home in a shopping bag."

"Somehow I don't see or hear a dear friend sitting across from me. Not to mention my AA sponsor."

"Did Novak tell you he chaired the committee that recruited the new Imam, who's in regular contact with radical clerics in Yemen and London? Sorry. I'll take a cup of your famous cappuccino. Let's dial this back, El. On second thought, how about a macchiato?"

Conte makes two macchiatos, which they take in silence. Martello thinks about the sandwiches. Conte breaks the silence.

"The hammer. You came here to act out the meaning of your surname. Mark the Hammer. Not in friendship. Mark the fucking Hammer."

"We're just talking, El. I need your help. If you have it, please turn it over. I leave, no consequences, end of story."

"Have it?"

"We believe you may have Mirko's computer."

"I don't."

"Don't force me to order a search of the premises. Within an hour this place is in shambles."

"Fuck it."

"Fuck it?"

"You people have already hacked into Mirko's computer, the Imam's computer."

"Robinson better not have told you this, Eliot."

"No comment."

"We're all over those computers. Sure. Problem is a forensic exam is necessary because everything dumped into the trash can itself be trashed, deleted, and only a forensic search into the hard drive can retrieve what the user is trying to hide. El, I need that computer."

"Mirko is conducting a clandestine romance, Mark. That's all it is."

"How do you know this?"

"No comment."

"El. Recall the bombing of the Fraunces Tavern near Wall Street, late seventies? Radical Puerto Rican nationalists?"

"No. That would be before you were born, Mark."

"We know all about Delores Delgado, do you?"

"Make your point, Mark."

"Her grandfather and great-uncle were the designers and executioners of the Fraunces Tavern bombing. Wall Street area. People died."

"You're losing it, Mark."

"Possibly. But if I'm not? You ready to take the consequences because you were blasé about connecting the dots?"

"What is Kyle saying about this?"

"We don't discuss this level of my work."

"Bullshit."

"I agree."

"Where does that leave us, Mark?"

"Okay. I'm going. On the way to headquarters I'm making a call. Count on it. I'm advising you."

"Go ahead. Advise me."

"Proceed as I do."

"How's that?"

"Exercising caution and due diligence."

Noon, and Conte's thoughts turn to sausage and peppers. He's eaten nothing for eighteen hours, since the tomato pie binge of the night before. She said afternoon, to collect her things. He'll sit at the desk, watch and wait. Conte has no appetite. Perhaps, maybe, a half sandwich at most. Or a quarter. Or none at all. He polishes off both sandwiches and a twelve-ounce bottle of Coke, and then the phone rings. She ignores his hello-with-a-mouthful. "Be there in an hour with Don Belmonte in his all-terrain vehicle. I have frightening news to report—tell you when I get there."

"Tell me now."

"Maureen Rintrona. Maureen. She's walking the dog this morning at dawn. A car pulls alongside, blasting Verdi. She thinks it was Verdi. The driver fires once at the beagle. The light was weak. We have almost nothing to go on."

"The dog? Not Maureen?"

"Yes."

"Killed the dog? They killed Aida?"

"Yes."

He flosses and brushes. Checks his hair in the bathroom mirror. Okay. Face—nothing to be done. Fifty minutes to go. Dusts and vacuums. Pacing again. Staring out again at quiet Mary Street. There. Angel again. Soccer ball again. Maneuvering in the snow. Dribbling east, whipping about on a dime, dribbling west.

Conte hadn't defined *o'scugnizzo* for her. The orphan boy living on the streets of Naples, by his wits. Poor, homeless, raggedly clothed. A rascal, a rapscallion. A scamp and a Devil. Angel, who insisted on pronouncing his own name the way a clueless English speaker would, *An-gell*, had never commented on Conte's proper Spanish rendition: *An-hel. An-hell?* Yes. Moreno the Anhellion. He must tell Catherine.

Mary Street's latest *o'scugnizzo*, and the son that Eliot never had.

CHAPTER 6

While Big Don Belmonte waits in the Wrangler, she tells Conte "I'm here now"—striding through the door toward the bedroom—"only to change into my favorite outfit and to propose that you and I meet to put our heads together as an investigating team and not necessarily for any other reason." It flashes through Conte's desperate mind that she could have proposed that they meet at The Florentine or The Chesterfield, they didn't have to meet here, unless … so why would she need to meet here in order to team up with me? …

"Even though," she says, "we have no evidence, we assume with confidence," following her into the bedroom, "that the shooter who tried to kill Bobby and the one who killed the dog are one and the same person."

In the bedroom, tight quarters, watching her take off her clothes, he says, "Your theory of the case"—panties and bra, God let her change those too—athletically fit, beautiful by anyone's definition—"sure, it's a good theory, Catherine, of course it is, probably it'll turn out to be the correct theory, I'd bet on it, sure, please take your panties off now."

"No."

From behind her, slips his hand inside the front of her panties. She freezes. She leans back into him.

"Nevertheless, Catherine, where's the hard evidence, putting this aside," touching his crotch.

She removes his moistened hand.

"Don is driving me down to Troy to talk to the lead detective on the case and—"

"Don off today?"

"No, but the all-too-kind Chief tells him he sympathizes how our feelings for Bobby—"

"All-too-kind."

"He tells Don do whatever to help."

Conte asks her in what sense they're a team, because what can he do, really, aside from "taking photos of cheating spouses in flagrante? A guy going down on his wife's best friend. For example."

Pulling on her form-fitting black leather pants, smoothing, stroking the wrinkles on her thigh, she says, "Let me elaborate the theory you're so high on."

"Hard on."

"Forget it, Eliot. The shootings. In Troy. They're tied to the murder of the Mafia hitter you described yesterday. I don't know how they're tied, but when I return tonight we're going over your story with a fine-tooth comb because—"

"Go over my story? My *story*? As if I'm a suspect of some kind?"

"As if you're a suspect of some kind. Yes."

"How nice, Catherine. In the meanwhile, Don is out there waiting and we could—"

Her blouse yet unbuttoned, small firm breasts big enough to (not quite) fit in your mouth, she says, "No. I'd like to, more than you might guess. No."

At the door, he stops her with, "What did you mean by 'not necessarily'?"

"Huh? What?"

"You said, 'not necessarily for any other reason.' Not necessarily means something else is not out of the question, doesn't it?"

"Forget the words, Eliot. You think too much about words. Because this is not about reading Melville. Even less about us having sex. This is about grooves and striations on bullets. This is about latent prints and indentations on shell casings. Think about a partial plate I.D. that places the vehicle in question maybe in Utica. These are the necessary things. Not us. Maybe never us."

He watches her go down the steps to the Wrangler, get in, do a fist bump with Belmonte, as Angel Moreno comes into view carrying a shovel to Conte's driveway. The crews had been at it all night and all day. The streets are in decent shape, the temperature at midafternoon has risen to the midforties and the worst December storm in fifty years is in retreat. The forecast for tomorrow: low sixties. Soon, the worst slush in fifty years. The promise of springlike weather triggers Conte's desire for his vegetable garden, buried under twenty-seven inches of snow.

Cruz and Belmont drive off down Wetmore. She doesn't look back—not even a wave. Conte goes out to Angel who tells him he'll dig out his car, because "Jefe needs wheels in his loneliness" and Conte replies, "If you wish, Angel, but I won't need my car. I'm taking a long walk alone. Alone is not the same as lonely, little man." Angel says, "Cool, big man," and begins to shovel out the driveway as if demonically possessed.

When he looks up, he catches sight of Conte half a block away and shouts, "Jefe, Angel don't asept a penny of the four hundred because you be like my uncle."

Walking west on Mary to the Bacon cross street and brooding on his destination. No hat, no boots. Prefers the punishment. Left at Bacon and two blocks south, rising to once-arrogant Rutger, where he turns right and west again—west to his destiny, but not all the way west to Rutger Park, near the city's center, where in the mid-nineteenth century Utica's original elite built ten-thousand-square-foot stone mansions, and then the less than rich, but rich enough, built stately five-thousand-square-footers of mere wood, somewhat east of Rutger Park in the early twentieth century, in the direction of the newly developed far East Side—newly saturated with immigrants from the south of Italy. He's muttering, he's scaring an African-American teenage girl carrying an infant, as he passes her, brushing elbows on the snow-narrowed sidewalk.

Shoes soaked through—uncomfortable but unconcerned because he's thinking about a drink. Why shouldn't he suffer? In the year since his children's murder on the West Coast and his father's death, he'd inherited a great sum that would permit him to purchase with ease several of the most expensive of the new homes high up on Valley View Road, at Utica's southern border—free of the sirens, the arsonists, the muggers desperate for a fix—he needs a drink very soon—this self-lacerating Conte is digging his fingernails into his long-ravaged cuticles, even now causing them to bleed as he pushes on toward Mohawk Street. He had refused the temptation to move on up. Believes he never felt the temptation. 1318 Mary would be home until the end—pushing hard now along Rutger, toes and ears numb, thinking in happy bitterness of the elite center at Rutger Park and its environs—all those condescending mansions now rundown, abandoned, or transformed to house the welfare class, the mentally cracked, and their good neighbors in the business of crime—brooding in a cold sweat with dry mouth—Rutger and Mohawk at last where his destiny yanks him up Mohawk toward South Street and the promised end: Barbone's Booze.

He sees them come pouring—they're pouring out of their homes and businesses—they're running toward South and the seven or eight police cruisers with their roof lights lit and spinning—they're gathering two blocks ahead at South, where uniformed men with billy clubs will keep them well back from the scene at the northeast corner of Mohawk and South. Barbone's Booze is cordoned off by the yellow barricade of crime scene tape. He's moving at a half jog, he falls twice on the ice, he's entering the crowd, the chatter, they killed, they robbed, who's safe anymore, these black animals, a matter of time, he have kids? Freddy? don't push me buddy, as Conte forces his way to the front, to the blank-faced officers Frick and Frack, lanky Ronald Crouse, who he doesn't know, and squat Victor Cazzamano, whose livelihood he'd saved several years ago in a nasty divorce case with interesting photos of his wife. They converse in whispers:

"Vic."

"Just between us, assume the black or P.R. element, you can't go wrong."

"Who's the lead detective?"

"Super Spic."

"Who would that be?"

"Holier-than-thou Men-fucking-doza." (Not a whisper.)

"Tino Mendoza?"

"I've already crossed the line."

"What happened?"

"No comment, they'll put my ass in a sling."

"You and Crouse first responders?"

"No comment, my ass et cetera."

"Give me a morsel, Vic."

"Massive blood."

"Freddy?"

"Does the bear shit in the woods? What brings you here anyway?"

"I was looking forward to a fifth of Johnnie Walker Black."

"Weird, Eliot."

"Weird how?"

"When me and Ronny enter, what do we find shattered on the floor, bottle of Johnnie Walker Black. Ronny runs out, the pussy, because he can't take the sight of Freddy. Me, after what you showed me the pictures of what my wife was doing, that cunt, I can take anything. So we right away get the call that this bastard Mendoza is coming to take over. So I see something on the floor that will interest Mendoza. So I take it, which he definitely could use in his investigation, because fuck him after the way he treats the uniforms."

"Johnnie Walker Black."

"Yeah. Now shake my hand."

Conte feels a small metal object on his palm. He pockets it.

"We all know you're in retirement as a P.I. That might induce a dramatic comeback in the bottom of the ninth."

"One more thing, Vic."

"My ass in a sling."

First a bowl of his homemade minestrone. Then a cup of hot chocolate, which he carries to the bathroom and places on the tub ledge alongside his cell and the casing of a spent bullet. He's hoping she'll give him an update from Troy. Almost asleep in the hot bath when it rings. Not her. Robinson:

"El. Serious news on the Ivanovic family. One of my uniform's cruising Bleecker this afternoon. He turns up Nichols where he spots a man and a woman escorted out of 608, where your Mirko lives, as you know. Three guys he never saw before with sunglasses. The man and the woman are cuffed."

"Mirko's parents you're saying?"

"We assume."

"My cruiser stops. My two uniforms get out. One of the sunglasses shows an I.D. My guys drive away."

"Martello's people, Robby?"

"The Imam is with Martello, Mirko is missing, and now Martello has the parents."

"What can you do about it, Robby?"

"Cocksuckers are a law unto themselves. They take them to a planet worse than Guantánamo."

"Christ."

"They don't give a shit what He fuckin' thinks, either."

(Long pause.)

"You still there, El?"

"Mirko."

"What about him?"

(Pause.)

"El, you still there?"

"I saw something today on South Street."

"Freddy Barbone, you referring to?"

"I am."

"Freddy was slaughtered, I mean slaughtered, El. One to the brain, which blows out the back of his head, and that's not the end of it. Then they almost severed off his head—it's attached by the skin at the back of his neck. Cash register is open and emptied out and a single bottle of scotch busted on the floor. A strange fact, but not according to Tino, who's got a theory."

"Are you free to tell me?"

"Tino's partner sees the open register and concludes a robbery motive, but Tino is a brilliant motherfucker. He notices Freddy's watch was apparently smashed in the event. Stopped at 9:17 last night. Freddy closes religiously at 8:15. Tino notices a key in the door."

"The robbery motive doesn't hold water, Robby. Somebody he knew. He's closed but opens up for a long-standing customer. Is that Tino's theory?"

"Welcome back, Detective Conte."

"Other bottles broken and strewn around?"

"Nope."

"So what we have here is a faked robbery motive by someone he lets in after hours, who shoots him and almost cuts off his head."

"A good old-time customer and a kind of friend, El, if we can imagine anyone befriending that asshole racist, for whom I fuckin' weep not, believe me."

"The savagery of the assault suggests—"

"Yeah. Total rage murder. They wanted to insult the corpse. What about the bottle of Johnnie Walker Black? What's your theory, El?"

"You son of a bitch. At the time I was at 608 Nichols Street. With Novak Ivanovic."

"Who the feds will not let give testimony, of course."

Conte says nothing.

"Curious, though, don't you think, El? Johnnie Walker Black. Like an obvious clue for those who knew your well-known drinking preference? This is a small town. Son of a well-known father. Booze bag, so on. You were Freddy's good customer at one time, as was his killer."

"A heavy-handed attempt at a setup. No one can take that seriously."

"But maybe someone wanting to point the finger at you and not so out of his mind that he forgets to pick up the shell casing."

"Forensically that would have been important, wouldn't it, Robby?"

"Shell casing or not, I have total faith in Tino."

"One thing we know for sure, Robby. Freddy would never let a black or a Puerto Rican in after hours. That's where he drew the line on his greed."

"Tino already came to that conclusion."

"Goodnight, Chief."

"Hold on, brother. I have something on the lighter side.

Milly comes home today, she tells me she sees Michael in the butcher shop at Hannaford's."

"Your former beloved assistant chief?"

"Yep. Michael Coca himself with a piece of frozen meat in his hand. He's staring at it. She buys lamb chops and when she leaves twenty minutes later, she passes the butcher shop again. He hasn't moved. He's still staring at the piece of meat in his hand. Milly says he always seems to be there when she shops on Tuesdays. The cashiers tell her Michael never buys meat and when he checks out it's with a single mushroom. They tell him a single mushroom is too light to register on the scale. He only says, 'I will pay top dollar.' Goodnight, El."

Knocks back half the hot chocolate. Resists, for the second time in two days, the temptation to call Catherine. Finishes off the hot chocolate—savoring in his imagination the rich aftertaste of a spiked drink. The shell casing in his palm. The language of indentations, for which Melville provides no help.

Runs water hot and long in the cooling bath. Slouches far down until his head, like a severed head, is afloat on the bubbled surface.

CHAPTER 7

He steps into the kitchen dripping from his bath, nude and spent. No word from Catherine of Troy. Peanut butter and crackers. Jelly sandwich—he cannot finish it. Twenty-ounce bottle of Coke—three sips. Handful of pistachio nuts and six spicy olives (*alla Siciliana*), followed by two antacid tablets, chewed slowly and savored.

Eliot Conte, solitary diner, had been an accomplished gourmet cook of Italian fare for Antonio Robinson as they listened, over the years, to Saturday afternoon broadcasts from the Metropolitan Opera, and an even more accomplished chef for Catherine Cruz since she'd moved in with him six months ago. But not for Robinson for the last six months, when they'd drifted apart, neither understanding why—neither willing to broach the subject of their quiet alienation following the settlement of his father's shockingly lucrative estate. Seventy-five percent to Conte, the son who'd been at odds with the father until the last two days of his life—several million plus the father's house on Catherine Street. Twenty-five percent to Robinson—was he harboring? was that it?—who promptly sold his modest house in shabby middle-class Deerfield Hills in North Utica, then purchased on the southern highlands of the Mohawk Valley, off Valley View Road, a $700,000 contemporary home on twenty acres, with a glass wall and a sweeping view of Utica below. Did he enjoy the view, Eliot wondered, while nursing a grudge over the division of the inheritance?

Conte in pajamas. Nothing to do but wait for Catherine's return from Troy, while working to distract himself from the waiting and the feeling inside the waiting that he is himself nothing, choked now by the fear that he would lose his new life as Catherine Cruz's housekeeper, cook, and proud gardener—lose Catherine herself and be dragged back to the Eliot Conte whose life before Catherine could not be called living. Flees the kitchen table to the couch, obsessively checking his watch, but time refuses to pass when she's gone. To the desk—fifteen seconds. Places watch in desk drawer. Stands in the middle of the room, floor gazing. Bedroom—her side of the bed—recalling the story of the ex-assistant chief Coca at the supermarket trying to buy a single mushroom and the report from the Unimpeachable Remo Martinelli of Coca on Bleecker, whacking the side of his nose with a popsicle stick, rhythmically and relentlessly whacking his nose bloody—a spectacle of irreversible insanity.

The couch again—reclining and retrieving the single positive of the last three terrible days: Angel Moreno ... he and Angel and Angel's parents in Cooperstown, two summers past ... Baseball Hall of Fame ... picnic, Otsego Lake ... on a perfect day in mid-July. Angel ... the unqualified good ... He awakes at 7:30 A.M. to find himself covered with an afghan, his head pillowed ... bracing odor of brewing coffee ... kneeling beside him, Catherine Cruz, who says:

"Hey."

"When did you get back?"

"You were asleep."

On his right side, elbow supported, he says: "Dressed to kill this early?"

"Coffee?"

"You see Bobby?"

"He's closing in on his old salty self."

"In other words, Catherine, he tells you to tell me to go fuck myself. In a loving manner."

"Yes."

"Did you tell him I told you the story?"

"No."

"He already assumed it?"

"Yes. Bacon and eggs?"

"Not hungry, Ms. Cruz."

"Me neither."

At the kitchen table, over coffee, he returns to her attire: "Going somewhere special this morning?"

"No."

"I don't believe you."

"El, the apartment above Tom Castellano's is for rent. Rutger and Culver."

"I know where it is. That's where the Mafia hitter lived. Going weird on me?"

"Tom told me because of what you did for him twenty years back, he's offering me the apartment at half the usual rent. 'On behalf of Eliot,' he says, 'who saved me from my cheating wife.' You'll have to tell me the story sometime. Rutger and Culver is no more than a ten minute walk—a two minute drive."

"We'll have physical proximity there?"

"Let's change this dangerous subject, Eliot."

"Spell out the details of dangerous. Slowly."

"Stop."

"Bobby know about his dog?"

"Not yet."

"The way he talked about that dog, Detective Cruz, you'd think—"

"It'll devastate him when Maureen tells him."

"What she should tell him, Catherine, somehow the dog got loose and was hit by a car. Let's call now and tell her that."

"What can you possibly be thinking, Eliot? The Rintrona family is in grave danger. She *has* to tell him. My former chief assigned a cruiser to the house 24/7."

"For how long? Forever?"

"Two weeks."

"Then what, Catherine?"

"We need to find the shooter. We have two weeks. Or shooters."

"*Shooters*? What d'ya mean? I'm driving down to see him after I get ready for the day."

"Go after lunch. He's got therapy this morning."

"Hear about Freddy Barbone?"

"Did we ever. Don got the call when we were talking to the top crime lab technician in Albany. Don struggled to hold back his pleasure."

"Freddy was an asshole."

"Our theory, El, a single gunman who did both Troy shootings?"

"An obvious true theory. I need more coffee."

"You're not crippled."

He fetches another cup. She refuses a refill.

She says, "The theory needs revisiting."

"You look like the cat that ate the canary."

"The crime lab in Albany compared shell casings recovered from both shootings. Different guns. Bullet fragments recovered: same story. Different guns. No question."

"So what? The shooter is a smart psycho. The theory is still good."

"The vehicles described by Bobby and Maureen—not even close to being similar."

"A very smart psycho."

"Who shoots the dog, El?"

"An extremely smart psycho, a diabolical bastard. He knows where the terror button is. Kill their dog and they'll crawl under the bed and never come out."

"*He*? When questioned, Bobby said he couldn't tell gender or race. Maureen says ditto except she adds that for some reason she leans toward female."

"Female so-called intuition?"

"I'm saying in a loving manner, El, go fuck yourself."

"I'd rather—"

"You've heard of the National Integrated Ballistic Information Network?"

"Bureau of Alcohol, Tobacco, and Firearms?"

"Yes. A database of over two million digital images of hard ballistic information gathered from crime scenes since the midnineties. The way it works, you digitally enter new crime scene ballistics into the system and in a matter of an hour or two you may get a hit. Meaning, what you entered seems to match ballistics derived from a prior crime scene, someplace else. The Albany lab got a hit, El. The guns identified were a Smith & Wesson M&P 9 millimeter and a Sig Sauer 1911 .45."

"Let me guess. These guns were used some time ago in crimes committed in Utica."

"Yes. And these guns were confiscated by Utica PD."

"But don't police departments destroy those guns?"

"Don says sometimes they're destroyed, sometimes they're auctioned off. But not immediately. An important fact. They're stored in the department basement until they have enough to auction or go through the trouble of sending them to a steel plant where they're melted."

"So there's a window of opportunity for someone inside to grab a gun or two. Who would have access to the storage unit?"

"Don is checking this morning on the two weapons linked to Utica. If they're still there."

"They can't be."

"Which means for sure, El, someone inside."

"Unless a cleaning—"

"Only high-level UPD personnel have keys to that area. According to Don."

"Definitively, then, Catherine. Someone inside. Has to be Antonio."

"You're leaping over a chasm now."

"Has to be, Catherine."

"Your female intuition, Professor Conte?"

"Of course. What else do we know?"

"Remember I said the database hit confirmed what seemed to be a match? To be certain the actual physical shell casings from the Troy shootings have to be compared under a microscope with the actual casings recovered from the Utica crimes. We have the Troy casings for a limited period. Don is thorough. He'll check if the guns in question are still there, and then he'll do the job that no one pays him for, which he's been doing on weekends for twelve years, since his wife died. Describing and logging all ballistic info from Utica crime scenes."

"There must be hundreds of shell casings he'd have to comb through before he finds the match."

"Don has a log and the patience of Job. It may take him a while, but he'll find the matching casings and then we'll know definitively."

Her cell. Don Belmonte, who tells her the weapons in question, according to the records clerk, were neither auctioned nor sent off for destruction. "And—ready for this? They're still there. In storage. I'm still working on the shell casings, Cath. Sometime this afternoon, the guns go to Syracuse for tests that determine if they've been recently fired, which we're confident they have. Hope to have the casings match tied up by noon."

Conte says, "This is beyond me," when she relays Belmonte's message. "This makes no sense on any level. Someone on the force contracts with someone to do these shootings? This someone on the force had some time ago pilfered the guns from storage for some possible, he knows not what, *future* action? This someone on the force hires an assassin to hit Bobby, or does it himself?"

"And then this engineer of violence, El, tells the would-be assassin to return the guns to him so that *he* can return them to storage where they've not been for several years. You said that the shooter was a smart psycho—"

"Extremely smart."

"You said he, she, whatever, was a diabolical bastard. Most criminals are fatally stupid, at the end of the day."

"Not this one, Catherine. This one is playing a game that I—I have no idea what game this one is playing."

"Bobby, Monday morning—the dog, Tuesday morning. Who else is in danger—it can't be the work of Antonio because if Antonio—it's obviously not Antonio. Because why would he put the guns back in storage?"

"Maybe we should add, Cruz, what happened Monday night. Freddy Barbone."

"Why? What does he have to do with Bobby and the dog? What possible pattern would Freddy fit into? Shooting from a car is one thing. It's antiseptic, sort of like high altitude bombing, but Freddy in the head at close range and then virtual decapitation, that's a very different M.O. That's not cold assassination. That's personal."

"What if inconsistency of M.O. is part of the plan? Let's think about that, Cruz. An effect of randomness, a deliberate performance of randomness and disconnection, which makes a coherent theory of these crimes impossible. I'm lost."

"Me too."

"So sit on my lap and we'll be lost together and talk about the first thing that comes up."

"First thing that comes up? Your juvenile idea of erotic humor?"

"Yes."

"Which you learned in the eighth grade?"

"Yes."

She's about to leave to sign the lease with Tom Castellano when he says, "Wait. I have something I'd like you to ask Don to check." He goes to the desk and returns with a small sealed envelope.

She opens the envelope: "Mind telling me where you got this?"

"After Don renders the verdict."

Albany. At Saint Jude, midafternoon. Seventh floor. The door to Rintrona's room is closed—a uniformed policeman sitting outside, who rises at Conte's approach.

"How are you, officer?

"Name?"

"Eliot Conte."

Checks clipboard: "Yeah."

Conte moves to enter.

"Hey! Did I let you in?"

"What's the problem, officer?"

"I'm the problem. Driver's?"

Officer looks at picture, looks at Conte, looks at picture, looks at Conte: "Yeah. Let me explain something, buddy. You don't just walk in for the simple reason the door is locked. The situation of security I'm up against? Life and death."

"I appreciate your service, officer."

"Check out with Sister Mary Ronald on the way out."

"Who's that?"

"Nurses' station down the hall. Don't play dumb. In her twenties. Audrey Hepburn."

"Officer, we're on the same page."

Steps into the room and freezes. Maureen, white as a sheet, by her husband, who's sobbing. The odor of all those flowers—twelve large bouquets arranged along the base of the walls—like those funeral parlors when he was young, Eliot with his father paying respect to the families and friends of deceased constituents. Heavy here with the same odor, sweet, at the edge of nauseating. Rintrona has a legal pad and ballpoint pen on his lap. He speaks with a hoarseness that Conte has never before heard:

"About time, you motherfucker."

Conte comes forward to the other side of the bed, facing Maureen.

Maureen says, "This language has to stop."

Rintrona says, "They killed my poor dog I loved, Maureen loved, fuckin' kids in the neighborhood loved. Who's next, Eliot?"

"Nobody's next."

"You stupid all of a sudden?"

"We'll get him soon."

"When? They let Maureen go for some reason. My daughter is next, that's who. Fuckin' throat is killing me."

Conte doesn't know how to respond.

Maureen says, "I can't sleep anymore."

Rintrona says, "We know who did this."

"Not yet."

"Stop bullshitting. My fuckin' throat. A catheter up my dick. Ever have a catheter up your dick?"

Maureen says, "Stop this language for once."

"What's the difference, Maureen? We're in the company

of our dear friend Eliot fuckin' Conte. My worthless dick. Secular nurse pulled it out the other day, I saw stars. She should have it up hers, then she'd know. Cunt. I get out of here—I can't talk no more, fuckin' Christ."

He writes on the legal pad: *Get out of here eventually I go to Utica kill that friend of yours. Fuckin swear to God.*

"Listen to me, Bobby. The odds are extremely against who you're thinking."

Maureen says, "Excuse me. I'm here too you know. Who is this person? We should go to the authorities with his name."

Rintrona writes and shows Maureen: *Once I get out and do the right thing then you know who this cocksucker is.*

Maureen says, "We don't have enough to deal with, Bobby? You have to become a vigilante off the deep end against this unknown person?"

Conte says, "Maureen is right."

Rintrona writes, *Who stops me?*

Maureen: "Jesus, Mary, and Joseph."

Conte then gives them the Troy ballistics findings. The difference of cars. He says, though not believing it, "Two different unrelated shooters."

Rintrona in a rage that brings searing pain to his throat, in a horrifying scream, "BALLS! BULLSHIT!" The pain drives him to tears and the groans of a dying animal. He writes: *Tell them the throat spray.*

Sister Mary Ronald appears. She says, "Open up for me, dear. I'm going to make you feel good." She sprays. Rintrona manages a smile. He writes her a note: *This thing they have up me down there. I'd like you to remove it so I can sleep in peace. Every time I move, that thing up me, I hit the ceiling. Please, Sister.*

"The secular's job, sweetheart."

He writes: *She's too rough. You.*

"I'm so sorry, Robert. I'll speak sternly to her."

He writes: *My life is in your hands. Call me Bobby.*

She suppresses a smile: "Call whenever you need me," and leaves.

"Good thing I'm not the jealous type, you old goat. A nun!"

Rintrona writes: *Takes me an hour to come these days. How about you?* Shows it to Conte, who says, "Forty-five minutes."

"What did you write that you don't show me? More filth?"

Rintrona whispers, "I'm afraid for my family and my life. I am afraid."

Maureen says, "I can't sleep, I can't eat, I can't sit still. Tomorrow we're sending our daughter to my sister in Minnesota. You never met Deirdre. She'll lose her job here. FIND THIS COCKSUCKER AND KILL HIM!"

The officer outside the door bursts in, gun drawn. Surveys the room. Points to Conte: "This guy a problem?" Rintrona signals all is well.

Conte decides to lie: "We have a very serious lead, not who you think, Bobby, and we're going to take care of this thing within two weeks. Catherine and I—we're close to cracking this thing. I promise."

Rintrona holds out his hand. Conte takes it in both of his. Then goes to the other side of bed and hugs Maureen, who says, "You promise two weeks?"

He says, "Yes. Or less. I'll be down again in a couple of days."

She says, "Wait—I'll go to the lobby with you because Bobby wants chocolate chip cookies. I told him twice they may not have chocolate chip—I told him I guarantee cookies but not chocolate chip. All right, Bobby?" Rintrona nods and smiles the smile of someone who has suffered soul-sucking damage.

In the elevator she presses the button not for the lobby but for the third floor, "We have to talk, Eliot." He nods. Maureen leads him to the dayroom and a quiet corner.

She says, "What I told that investigating detective? Opera music? I held it back from Bobby, and you have to promise you'll never tell him because the killing of Aida, it was worse in his mind than the bullets he took. If I tell him opera, Verdi, I can't predict what it'll do to him."

"I promise."

"The last four years it's opera, it's the dog, whose name I don't agree with, by the way, and I don't come into the picture except here and there. I cook."

"I'm sorry, Maureen, but I know he loves you. Very much."

"How do you know?"

"Trust me on that, but forgive me—I have to change the subject. It was opera from the shooter's car? For sure?"

"Pretty sure. I'm not like you and Bobby, a fanatic. I like it sometimes well enough, but what do I know? Nothing. Last year he took me to *La Bohème* at the Met. Four hundred for two tickets plus dinner and taxis. What happens twice, during the love duets? I fall asleep. He gives me the elbow. After, he said I hurt his feelings. Then he won't talk for a week."

"Bobby's sensitive about love duets. You heard Verdi?"

"Just guessing. It reminded me of what he plays at home,

which is usually Verdi—which I usually tune out because I have a lot on my mind, Eliot."

"Maureen, we have so little to go on. This could be important. Bear with me. Vocal or orchestral?"

"Vocal."

"A chorus or one or two singers?"

"One."

"Male or female?"

"Male."

"Tenor? Baritone? Bass?"

"Tenor, for sure."

"Good. Was the music slow and moody or fast and agitated?"

"Fast and agitated."

"Good. Sing some of it."

"Have you lost your mind? Are you out of your mind?"

"Try. Please."

"Da da da daaah. That's all I remember. It sticks in my mind for some reason."

He tries to imitate.

"No. The notes start high and go down one step at a time, if you know what I mean."

"Like this?"

"No offense. You're a little flat."

"Like this?"

"Sort of, but you have to hold onto the last one. Like this."

"Does it remind you of anything Bobby plays at home?"

"He plays it so loud I go to the mall whenever possible and I take Aida with me because I'm afraid it'll hurt her ears permanently. Did you know dogs have five hundred times more sensitive ears than we do?"

"I didn't."

"Can you imagine what she hears when he plays that stuff?"

"I can only imagine."

In the lobby, he says, "If you think of anything else, get in touch as soon as you can."

"I will. Promise not to mention this to my husband?"

"Promise." (Thinking, Unless I must.)

In the parking lot, Conte inserts a CD —choruses from Verdi's operas. On the Thruway home, the long descent into the Mohawk Valley, he feels his cell vibrate in his coat pocket. Turns off the music. Catherine:

"Almost home?"

"Twenty minutes."

"Don has interesting news. That shell casing you gave me?"

"Tell me."

"It matches the one from the Sig Sauer that killed Bobby's dog. So what we obviously want to know, as soon as you arrive, without delay, Eliot, I'm warning you as an officer of the law, where did you get it? Don and I are waiting for you. At 1318 Mary."

"Can't wait to see you both."

The music again. Chorus of the Hebrew Slaves from *Nabucco*: "Va, pensiero." (Go, worries.) What did Maureen hear blasting from the shooter's car? What exactly from Verdi? If it was Verdi.

CHAPTER 8

The tiny Vietnamese tollbooth clerk at the North Utica exit informs him that he's just received word—the bridge over the New York Central train yard on Genesee Street is blocked in both directions by a gasoline-spewing, jackknifed tractor trailer. Conte's direct route home to endure the music of interrogation now impossible, he deviates to the west side of town in the grip of the old desire—he deviates to the hip Varick Street bar scene situated at the edge of dilapidated Polish Town—all Poles long since scattered to the suburbs and the south of Florida. Varick Street—deserted in a sudden hard rain—the street dangerously puddled and slushed—the temperature freakishly hovering in the midsixties—and now, in mid-December, at this latitude, just two days after a record snowstorm, rolling thunder.

Pulls over to The Gay Martini. Steps ankle deep but unperturbed through a puddle and strides to the bar. Knows what he's doing. This time, without illusions. This time, no excuses.

"Not open till seven, Dad."

The bartender polishing glasses is a pretty twenty something—even with, especially with? the diamond stud in her cheek. He's surprised. Finds it unexpectedly sexy.

Lays down a twenty: "The door's open. You're here. I'm here. Double Johnnie Black, straight up, keep the change."

"No can do, sir."

Sir. He knows what that means. You're old. Older than "Dad." Varick Street misfit. Scram, Eliot.

"Please."

She shakes her head sadly. She's seen it many times—a dry alcoholic on the verge. She leans on the bar, close to him: "You're strong when you want to be." Softly: "Don't you want to be? Big guy?"

Leaning into her fragrance: "May I ask you a question?"

"No can do. I'm in a long-term relationship."

Stepping back, flushed with embarrassment: "No. Not that." (Forced smile.) "I mean, is this a gay bar?"

"You mean strictly?"

"Yes."

"Dude, there is no more 'strictly.' "

Out of nowhere, a warm wave of relaxation washes over him and a grin, ear to ear, not seen on the Conte visage for months, as his desire to drink is extinguished for a while. He likes her. Wants her to like him. (Just "like," that's all.) Turns and starts to walk away when she stops him with: "You're not that old looking, you know. Really, you're really not. You could be considered an attractive father-figure option in some quarters." Conte wonders, In which quarters? In what possible world? Hers? Absurd.

At the door, turning back to her, that grin again: "I'm fifty-six."

Coming over to him: "I'm twenty-eight, big deal. It's all

relative." She hands him the twenty, winks, says, "I'll take a rain check, Daddy."

He puts the twenty in his wallet and removes his defunct business card:

ELIOT CONTE, PRIVATE INVESTIGATOR
1318 MARY STREET
moby@gmail.com

Writes in his cell number on the card: "If you ever have the kind of trouble the police have no interest in pursuing, give me a call, angel."

"Couldn't afford you, Pops."

"You can. You'd be redeeming the rain check."

She looks at the card again for a long moment and replies, "Would you by any chance be related to—"

"Yes. But not by chance."

She points to the street: "The storm passed. Feeling better?" He suppresses an urge.

"Don't lose the card, angel. I owe you."

In the vicinity of Rutger Park, a stone-packed snowball thuds against and cracks the passenger side window of his nine-year-old Toyota Camry. Skinny teenage male, white, arms akimbo, sneering, sagging pants. Conte rolls down the window. Sagging pants says, "Bring it on, Gramps." Conte considers the offer with surging pleasure. The kid gives him the finger. Conte shouts, "I'm making progress, asshole," and drives off.

Home, in the driveway, calls Anthony Senzalma.

"Dinner at 8? Joey's? It's crucial."

"With pleasure, Eliot, as always."

Calls Joey's and makes the usual unusual request, invariably granted, to sit not in the dining area, where Senzalma feels vulnerable, but in the cramped office behind the kitchen.

Inhales it as he opens the door—sautéing garlic. She's making the sauce of garlic and olive oil, simple, even I can do it, Catherine said shortly after she moved in, who was not in his league as a cook—in truth, she was not much good at all as a cook, though it was a truth never uttered, except by her, though she tried and made many disasters, which he always pronounced very good. He lets her make breakfast, always, because anybody can make oatmeal in the microwave, or pour cold cereal into a bowl and start the coffee, and she throws mediocre sandwiches together with the best of them.

Walks in quietly. Can see her in the kitchen—her back to him. He'd warned her how many times? Lock up when I'm away, the neighborhood is changing, but with Big Don Belmonte here, no need, maybe. Where was Big Don? She doesn't hear him enter—radio, open door. What does he have to do to bring her to her senses? He sings out with the old mocking tone, "Honey! I'm home!"

She turns: The spontaneous smile that brings the sun, quickly shut down.

"I expected you a lot sooner."

"Where's Don? Be careful that garlic doesn't blacken."

"Have I ever let the garlic go black and bitter? Don got a call from the Chief to report immediately to the Chief's house. An hour ago."

"Reason?"

"Antonio wouldn't give one over the phone. I made enough for the two of us."

"The garlic—"

"I know what I'm doing. Do you? Where were you, if I may ask?"

Takes saucepan off burner.

"Your last supper or mine?"

"Don't change the subject. What kept you?"

"I'll sit with you, but I have plans for dinner."

"So what kept you?" Her suspicion is palpable.

"Let me drain the pasta. Sit. I'll take care of the rest."

She sits—he serves.

"I'm very sorry, Eliot. It somehow slipped my mind that you don't know Russian. Let me spell it out in English: What kept you?"

"Varick Street."

Puts her fork down. Chews and swallows:

"You fell off the—"

"We don't say that anymore if you're *in* The Program. They only say that in the movies. We, in The fucking Program, say, I went *out*. You want to know if I went *out*?"

"Did you?"

"I went to Varick Street for the purpose of going *out*. Yes."

"And you went out?"

"I definitely got my feet wet."

"Spit it out, Eliot. You slipped."

"I walked into a deep puddle, that's what I did."

"You're telling me you had quite a few?"

He takes off his shoes and socks and in his big, powerful hands wrings them out on the floor.

"Did you or did you not drink?"

"I was saved by my guardian angel."

"You're drunk."

"Not a drop. The bartender was my guardian angel."

"Suddenly you're an old-time Catholic?"

"Bred in the bone."

"Was she good-looking?"

"Who said she?"

"I did."

"She was young, she was kind, and she distracted me from myself and what I wanted to do."

"Distracted how? Do I want to know?"

"No idea. I wanted one bad. Then I didn't want one."

"She charmed you."

"Good thing you're not the jealous type."

"Says who?"

"Eat your pasta, Catherine, before it cools off, and next time consider adding parsley in with the sautéing garlic and some flakes of chili pepper. If you're cooking for yourself, lots more black pepper. If for me too, hold the black pepper or I'll pee every ten minutes for a week."

"Thank you, Chef. Having dinner with the bartender?"

"Anthony Senzalma."

"That what she calls herself?"

"Really. Anthony. At Joey's."

"What you two have in common beats the hell out of me."

He reaches across the table and takes her hand.

"I was saved by my guardian angel's youthful kindness."

"I'm pretty young. I try to be kind."

"You are pretty, you are young, and you are always kind."

"Where did you get it?"

"What?"

"Don't play games. The shell casing. We have to know."

"Somebody gave it to me."

"Stop this game."

"I'll never tell, but I will tell you where this party found it."

"I'm all ears."

"In the vicinity of Freddy Barbone's blasted head."

"You cannot be serious."

"I just told you a fact, Catherine."

"Wait till Don hears this."

He pulls her plate and fork over and starts in on the pasta.

"What exactly do you think I've just told you, Catherine?"

"Same person who shot Bobby's dog. Obviously."

He savors. He swallows:

"Same gun, sure. Not necessarily same shooter. That conclusion won't hold up, ladies and gentlemen of the jury. Because, as you've heard, that particular weapon was located in the Utica PD headquarters' storage, where any number of noble officers of the law have access." (Pointing his fork:) "You agree?"

"Yes. Now give me the normal human opinion rather than the pitch of a soulless lawyer."

"Where's the irrefutable linkage of gun and shooter? Okay, okay. Totally likely the same shooter, but no proof yet that it was and who would have the motive to kill a dog and then Freddy? How are they connected, if they are?"

"Both dogs?"

"Very nice, Catherine."

"What do you always tell me? Humor knows no pieties? Our only weapon against the dark?"

"Forget it, Catherine. What's the connection of those two shootings with the shooting of Bobby Rintrona? If there is one."

Her cell. Belmonte. She listens without responding until the end, when she says, "This is insane."

"What is insane?"

"Antonio called him to the house because—they have a Jack Russell terrier, named Jack Russell, did you know that, Eliot?"

"They don't *have* one, Catherine. They *had* one. Isn't that what you're going to tell me?"

"Milly's walking him. They're in the driveway—no, I mean *she*'s in the driveway and the dog's in the snow-covered lawn area on one of those retractable leashes that allows the dog—there was a shot. The dog's head exploded. Something else. Worse. Apparently the bullet, which passed through the—it must have ricocheted off the driveway because Milly—a fragment shattered her knee. She's at Saint Elizabeth's where Don talked to her. Antonio is adamant. None of this gets out to the public."

"What did she tell Don about what she saw?"

"Nothing. No car. No drive-by. Nobody around. Don concludes high-powered rifle with a scope from somewhere on the hill across from the driveway. No witnesses.

No neighbors. Don says it would be highly unlikely to find a shell casing because the shooter, if he didn't pick it up, fired from wooded and brushy terrain, and it would take many men scouring foot by foot in the deep snow and anyway Antonio wants this thing kept secret for some reason."

"If Don's right—"

"Don's always right, El."

"A precision shot intended for the dog's head. The shooter could easily have killed Milly, but didn't want to. Where was Antonio when the shooting occurred?"

"Don didn't say. Why?"

"If he's at home, he's in the clear."

"You cannot be serious."

"Call Don, tell him to pin that down. How did Antonio learn of the shooting is the point."

"You actually think—"

"Rule nothing out in advance. Isn't that what you've taught me, Detective Cruz? Motive—Jesus, I have no clue. Kill his own dog? Put his wife in danger?"

"See the pattern, connect the shootings, Detective Conte. Tie irrefutable forensics to a subject who will never take the stand. The D.A. invents motive. Because the jury wants a story. Motive is beside the point except in those bullshit novels of the courtroom."

"Motive is totally irrelevant to the real-life police work of solving crimes? You can't mean that, Catherine."

"Largely irrelevant. The pattern. The forensics. Plus one other thing: luck. Let's review the facts."

"Okay: Bobby. Three from a car. What does three tell us, Catherine, if not that the shooter intended murder?"

"What else it tells, El, he, or she, whatever, was not that good with a handgun. It's hard, very hard, to be accurate with a handgun unless you have a lot of practice."

"Wait. Not necessarily. Maybe the shooter *was* good with a handgun on the practice range with a paper target. But with an actual human target, for the first time, he loses his composure. He's like a first-time deer hunter with buck fever when the buck crosses his path, which he can't hit no matter how close."

"Which leaves us at square one."

"The killer of Bobby's dog, though. Bing! One shot."

"What we know about Troy, El: two different guns, two different cars. But likely same shooter because no other theory makes sense. Day one, Bobby. Day two, his dog. Same shooter, El. Has to be."

"Who suddenly becomes a deadly marksman?"

"No, El. Who gets lucky with the handgun, but whose target is obviously the dog, lucky or not."

"Okay, Freddy Barbone. Head shot up close. Someone he knows, he lets in after hours. Rock solid theory, no?"

"Rock solid, even though there is no such thing."

"The virtual decapitation?"

"Rage murder, Mr. Conte. Someone who secretly hates Freddy."

"The Robinsons' dog. Has to be the shooter who did Bobby's dog. Has to be."

"Who's not that good with a handgun and knows it. But a high-powered rifle with a properly calibrated scope—we say 'has to be,' El, when we *know* nothing. Anybody with minimal long-gun experience can be deadly with a properly calibrated scope. Anyone with some hunting experience. You're going out to dinner and you just ate half of my—"

"Okay. If the same shooter in all cases, Catherine, then each of the targets has something in common with the others." Pushes the plate back to her.

"If the same shooter, then Freddy—what, my sauce is bland?"

"Freddy has something in common with Bobby? I'm in the dark."

"Yes, Eliot. If the same shooter." Pushes the plate back to him. "My sauce is lousy?"

"And they each have something in common with the dogs?" (He laughs.)

She's suppressing a smile: "Absolutely."

"If we had a motive, we could find common ground."

"Ass-backwards, El. The ballistic linkage of Bobby and Freddy gives us eventually a prime suspect and a twisted motive in some sick psychological underground. We have a likely killer. The pattern and the forensics give us the real killer, not the likely one. Motive? Who cares at that point?"

"A lot depends on Antonio's whereabouts, if they can be innocently accounted for. I can think of two theories, mutually exclusive, depending on—"

(The doorbell.)

"Saved by the bell, El, because we're still at square one. We have nothing."

Angel Moreno. Conte invites him in:

"No way, Jefe."

"In a big hurry, Angel?"

"Otherwise engaged, yeah."

"Santa's watching, Angel. Are you naughty or nice?"

"Christmas shopping. Last-minute anxiety, Jefe."

"You have money for that?"

"Strictly online, big man, the new American way."

"That requires—"

"Yeah. Credit card."

"Obviously, you don't have a credit card."

"You got that right, señor."

"I don't like the implication, Angel."

"Yeah."

"Why did you knock on the door?"

"I been hackivatin' on your behalf. That Mirko the Bosnian did something stupid. Got married in Syracuse."

"Can't tell you how relieved I am to hear that news. Thank you, Angel."

"I don't disrespect marriage all three genders every which way, Jefe, but fuckin' *Syracuse*? Know where I'm at?"

"I do."

Glancing to the kitchen. "I see the fox of all foxes is back. She be *La Jefa* over your ass." She waves to him. "I think she like me. Beware of the young male stud, Jefe."

"You're still thirteen, Angel?"

"Don't take me and the fox lightly, man."

Conte laughs.

"Think I'm a clown, Jefe?"

"I think you're the best. No one in your league, Angel."

"Yeah. One other thing. That Martello groper? He's lunching with Congressman Kingwood hush hush concerning the drama of Sunday."

"They said drama?"

"Kingwood said that word, which I analyze as bullshit on Sunday, no disrespect to the legitimate theater. Give *La Jefa* my love. See! She be blowing me a kiss. She already make her choice."

"Wait. What about you, your Dad, and me go bowling sometime over the holidays?"

"All due respect to the proletariat, but Angel Moreno don't feature working-class recreations." He goes.

She says, "Where that kid came from only God knows."

"Literally. Listen. I've got to leave soon. Where are we with our so-called theory?"

"We have no theory. All I can think of is tell our friends with dogs, 'potty train your dog.' "

"Kyle and Mark have a dog."

"So does Tom Castellano."

On the way to Joey's, Catherine's words keep repeating in his head. Tell our friends … potty train your dog. Our friends. *We*, the link? The figure in the carpet? But Freddy was no friend … Punch a brick wall, Eliot. Where's your guardian angel? What's her name?

He pulls over, makes a call:

"Tony, Eliot. You at Joey's?"

"Where else would I be?"

"Just making sure."

"You don't sound like yourself, El."

(The ghosts of his murdered daughters grip his throat.)

"El, you still there?"

"Just making sure, Tony."

He drives off only to stop in the middle of the next block to make another call. This one not in anxiety, but with cold calculation:

"Robby, it's me."

"Yeah."

"Milly's birthday—Jeez, it slipped my mind. I'd like to wish her belated felicitations. How's she doing? It's been a while."

"She's in Florida for the holidays."

"Oh ... so how was your day, Robby? How's it going, man?"

"I hardly ever hear from you anymore, and you're asking me about my fuckin' *day*? Milly's birthday was a month ago, which you never forgot for ten years and you didn't forget this time either because you sent a card a month ago. Stop bullshitting me."

"Jeez, my memory's gone to the dogs. Maybe the incomparable Jack Russell the Jack Russell would be willing to give it back to me."

(Silence.)

"Come on, Robby, don't you think that was somewhat witty? That little dog Milly's so crazy about is a real sweetheart. And smart? I never saw smarter."

"Why did you call?"

"Just wanted to talk. I miss us. Don't you?"

"Sure."

"The opera on Saturday afternoons—just us two—the amazing sandwiches Milly put together. They're doing *Il Trovatore* this Saturday with Anna Netrebko. Remember that sultry Russian beauty? We saw her in *Lucia*. A voice like that, you said, pouring from that body? You said it was better than the best sex. You said it was like her voice was doing you. Let's go down to Troy for the high-def broadcast. What d'ya say?"

"I doubt it."

"What d'ya say this summer we resume the varmit hunting we did in high school? Remember the fun we used to have? The rats at the dump, big as cats? Jeez! What an amazing deadeye you were, Robby!"

(No response.)

"Remember that time we took our father's .22 Hornet up to Smith Hill? Near the TV Towers? We took little Tony Senzalma, who's shaking like a leaf in the backseat near that souped-up .22 with the zeroed-in scope. Bullets the size that dwarf normal .22 bullets. Like a .30 caliber. Deer ordnance. Assassination ordnance, you might say. And I'm driving and I spot a woodchuck fifty yards out and stop the car and you're about to get out with the rifle—what did I tell you? Do you remember?"

"Fuckin' roly-poly cocksuckers are too smart, you said. They hear the car door open and run down to their underground apartments. Then you said—"

"I don't believe I spoke so obscenely. Roll down the window, Robby, is what I said. And you did. You didn't get out. You rested the barrel on the doorframe. Boom! Right through the head. You were always a great head shooter, it was your specialty, the head shot, and it was the biggest one we ever saw. Remember little Tony's reaction?"

"He cried."

"We stretched that thing out on the sidewalk in front of our father's house and his length ran the entire width of the sidewalk. He had to weigh thirty-five pounds, at least. He was growing huge with impunity up there because no one ever shoots a rifle within city limits unless—you still there, Robby?"

"Unless? Unless *what*?"

"Silvio willed that rifle to you in honor of your superior marksmanship. You still have it, I presume?"

"Yeah, and fuck your presume."

"Something wrong, Robby?"

"Like you care. I'm coming down with something. I need to go to bed."

"Give Milly my love. Hope she's in tip-top these days."

(No response.)

"You have my love too—despite whatever."

"I'm hanging up."

"One more thing, Robby."

(Line goes dead.)

CHAPTER 9

Anthony V. Senzalma picks unhappily at a plate of small, spicy-hot sausages, as he awaits Eliot Conte in Joey's office, in the uncommunicative company of bodyguard #1—a slim, stern-faced African-American dressed in a form-hugging, custom-made Italian suit with a .44 Magnum, long barreled and silencer equipped, resting in her lap. For the duration of the dinner, Geraldine Williams will not take her eyes off Conte, whom she had judged correctly, six months ago, to be unstable.

The Giant of Mary Street, as Senzalma thinks of him, parks behind the restaurant and hurries through a sudden cutting wind and steeply plunging temperature to a door alongside a large, stinking garbage dumpster. Waiting for him, as usual, in a surgical mask, is bodyguard #2, Dragan Kovac, a Bosnian immigrant of sumo-wrestler build. The big Bosnian says, "How's it going?" Conte replies, "Good, and you?" as the Bosnian frisks him, though in desultory fashion.

Conte enters, is met by bodyguard #1 who frisks him again, this time rough and shameless over every inch of his body. She says, "Shoes." He complies. She puts them out of reach. The odd couple, Conte and Senzalma, embrace, take their seats at the desk, Senzalma behind, Conte in front, with his back to bodyguard #1, who sits in a far corner. Conte turns to her—it's a ritual moment with them—says, "You'll make some guy happy with that big thing in your lap, Geraldine." According to script, she replies with a nod and the smallest trace of a smile.

Six months ago the fire-breathing right-wing talk radio host had knocked on Conte's door after dark, in the company of his bodyguards, and said, "I've come in long overdue gratitude." After a thirty-year hiatus in their friendship, Senzalma suggests they get together regularly. The apolitical Conte, who couldn't help tuning in daily to Senzalma's show, surprised himself by agreeing to the proposal that they meet soon at Joey's, in clandestine fashion. Senzalma was an irresistible abomination.

That startling moment at Conte's front door marked the unlikely resumption of an unlikely friendship, dating back to their freshman year at Proctor High, when the respected and feared son of Silvio Conte took pity on the slight and bespectacled Anthony, who in a school of working-class tough guys brought derision, shoves, and sharp elbows upon himself by insisting on carrying his books in a yellow briefcase. Conte's friendship insured protection, and from the day that star halfback Antonio Robinson was seen eating lunch with his best friend Eliot and little Anthony, little Anthony became himself a person to be feared and catered to. Then it ended, their Proctor High idyll: Antonio won a scholarship to play football at Syracuse, Eliot went off to Hamilton College, little Anthony, more painfully alone than ever, enrolled at Utica College, never to leave his hometown—because no one ever loved Utica more, or dreamed so grandly of restoring the city to its former glory.

Years later, at the peak of his notoriety, with lucrative offers to speak pouring in, Senzalma refused them all with a simple note, "I am rooted like the elegant Elms that once graced my sad city." When the president of Yale's Young Republicans replied with the reminder that Dutch Elm disease had killed off ninety-eight percent of America's elms, "Wake up and smell the coffee, Guido," Senzalma replied back, "You call yourself conservative?" Though stung by the implication that he was living in hopeless nostalgia, the condescending message from the Yalie inspired a dream that Senzalma knew he alone among Uticans could make real, if only he could enlist the help of Eliot Conte, whose discretion he could count on.

At their first dinner, Senzalma quickly disarmed the uneasy Giant of Mary Street. Sure, he said, he was earning $40 million a year and had recently signed a two-book contract with Knopf for an advance in seven figures. In the talk radio hierarchy, he drew a daily audience twice that of the former King of Talk Radio, the celebrity he referred to as Rushing Lintballs. As they shared an antipasto for two that would have fed four, with a forkful of prosciutto poised at his mouth Senzalma reached down into his briefcase and laid a stack of documents before Eliot to prove that his right-wing hate rhetoric was ("if I may say so, Eliot") one of the great hoaxes in mass media history. Letters of gratitude, addressed to a famous lawyer in D.C., clipped to bank transfers, thanking the attorney for his anonymous client's very substantial gifts to Planned Parenthood, the NAACP, Greenpeace, the National

Organization for Women, and the National Confederation of Lesbians, Gays, Bisexuals, Transgenders, and Secure Big Straight Males.

Conte had asked at that first dinner, "Why reveal this to me? Now? Why me?"

"Because deep friendship requires honesty. I have no friends."

Conte then placed his hand on Senzalma's and said, "What has changed? The sweet little guy I knew at Proctor is still a sweet little guy. Your public posture is an act, good, but your true politics is of no interest to me. Tony, you're wealthy beyond all need and all eventualities. Why not just quit and come out of the left-wing closet?"

Senzalma replied with instant passion, leaning in, "Because there is no greater pleasure for me than to play the Devil. I steal from the Devil in order to give to the angels."

The wind rattles the window. The building shakes. The big Bosnian enters and says, "Can I stay in tonight? It's bad out."

Senzalma replies like a disapproving parent, "Dragan, didn't I tell you to wear your heavy coat—didn't I tell you twice?" Dragan goes back out.

Eliot says, "Fuckin' weather is out of its mind lately."

"Utica, Eliot, just Utica."

The willowy knockout Raymona enters, "The usual, boys?" They nod.

Senzalma watches her out the door. He's in the room, but not in the room. Eliot says, "Come back, Tony, she's gone."

"Unfortunately."

"What else is on your mind, Tony?"

"Tonight you called, Eliot, to arrange a last-minute dinner—you never call to initiate, not once. It's taking over your mind again. Isn't it? The tragedy of your children."

"Let's eat first."

"What you wish to confide in me would spoil our meal?"

"Let's change the subject, shall we?"

"Freddy Barbone! My Lord! The news made the *Times*. The details of what they did—granted he was not a lovable person. Nevertheless."

"He was a pig."

"He deserved mercy, Eliot."

"No he didn't."

"Everyone deserves mercy."

"Not in my book."

"When you carry the name Barbone, you certainly do. Senzalma! Imagine being called Anthony without-a-soul. I'm still not over it."

"Tony Senz, that's what Robby and I called you. Sometimes Tony Terrific."

"And a burden was lifted. I felt rebaptized."

"Tony Senz. Tony Terrific."

Senzalma grins.

"The speculation, Eliot, is that Freddy was connected and went the way of his father and uncle, but the details sound to me like an emotional extremist, not a professional of the underworld."

"Your father's brother in Philly, didn't you tell me in our Proctor days he was a pro of that kind?"

"Don't remind me."

"Still alive?"

"Oh, yes, and still active, according to his daughter."

"In touch with him?"

"Please."

"Happen to know where he resides?"

"No. Sandra, of course, does."

"How old is he?"

"Mid-eighties. Maybe more. Excuse me, Eliot, why all this curiosity about this awful person?"

"Want to move on to another topic, Senz?"

"As fast as possible."

Raymona pokes her head in. "I forgot to ask about drinks. The usual?" They nod.

Senzalma watches her out again.

"Carlo. Isn't that his name?"

"Yes, Eliot."

"Sandra must have moved as far from Philly as possible."

"She stayed. Never married and moved in with him after her mother passed. This is not a change of subject. What's on your mind? I'm beginning to have a terrible inkling."

"After we eat."

Raymona enters with a carafe of ice water and two glasses. Says she'll be back in a minute with the food.

Senzalma says, "Thank you, dear."

She smiles, warmly, genuinely, "You're welcome, sweetie." Leaves.

Conte says, "I know how much you love your glass of wine."

"I do, but I wish to support your long journey of sobriety. For all you know, I have a drinking problem of my own up in my jail on Smith Hill."

Raymona returns pulling a food cart: Big bowls of calamari and Utica Greens. A salad for two of tomatoes, cucumbers, cherry peppers, onions. Full orders of eggplant parmigiana, pasta fagioli and meatballs, veal saltimbocca, jumbo shrimp scampi, Utica Riggies. And a hot loaf of bread (made on the premises).

She says, "Be careful you guys don't give yourselves an attack. I doubt our insurance covers it."

"We're nibblers, Ray," Eliot says.

"Mona, we're doing Italian dim sum," Anthony says.

"You guys! I love you both."

She exits. Senzalma says, "I really go for her, Eliot, I really do. Do you think she goes for me?"

"She's married."

"Relevance in our day and age?"

"Raymona and Michael are obviously happy."

"You and Catherine happy?"

"Let's enjoy this, Tony. Let's eat and talk about something else."

"I'm lonely, Eliot."

"I know, Anthony."

Neither eats.

Senzalma takes a card from his jacket, slides it over to Conte and says, "This is the subject I had hoped would occupy us tonight."

"This postcard? In sepia?"

"Taken in 1907. What do you see?"

"A street with big trees on either side."

"Not any street. Rutger. The camera looking due east from Rutger Park. In those days, it was called Rutger Place.

Not any trees, either. Elms in the glory of their full maturity. Those big boughs—see how they arch up and over on both sides of the street! Up in the upper half they touch and intertwine like gentle lovers. These trunks and these boughs," caressing the postcard, "sleek, they're svelte, just like—"

"How can I help, Senz? Just say the word."

"We're looking east down a long, leafy elm tunnel. Way up, a hundred feet high, they make a—not a roof. What would you call it?"

"An arch."

"Another word is on the tip of my tongue."

"Canopy?"

"Yes! Sheltering and enclosing the humanity beneath."

"The humanity? You're referring to those pseudo-aristocrats who ruled this city in the nineteenth century from Rutger Park and showed no humanity to the new immigrants—to our people? They're dead like all the elms that were wiped out by Dutch Elm disease. They had money, Senz. That's all they had. Money."

"They also had a way of life. Big houses. Big property. Sure. And big gardens. That's the thing. Grapevines. Fruit trees. Apples, peaches, and plums all big and juicy. Vegetables galore. Rutger Place was an ethnic neighborhood of English-Dutch stock. Aside from the wealth, not much different from the East Utica way of life we grew up in and loved. Our culture."

"Tony Terrific. (Pause.) You have gone insane."

"Why did they call it Rutger *Place*? Do you know? Because it was a *place*! *This* place is not *that* place! That's what a place is. A different thing—a little world. Those people you scorn rooted themselves there, and the place eventually owned them as much as they owned the place. Visiting each other's houses—going to the same churches—riding their bicycles built for two along Rutger in their bonnets with long colorful ribbons streaming behind them in the wind. What held them together as a neighborhood was an idea of the good life, which because they shared it, they never had to discuss and argue about it."

"You're barely alive in the present with your hidden life—you're a hermit, Senz, thinking about the past and dreaming about Raymona who will not be in your future. You have a view of Utica, up there on the hill, but Utica has no view of you."

"The East Side when we were young—we had the elms too. Don't laugh! Your Mary Street had the elms. Sure, our houses and backyards were tiny in comparison, but we had the gardens—the vegetables and the grapevines and the fruit trees. There was a story about a man named Tomaso, who once lived at 1303 Mary. We all heard it growing up. He had a cherry tree the size nobody ever saw or heard of before or since."

"You're flying high, Senz. A controlled substance?"

"We walked around the block—we visited each other on our front porches in good weather—we talked on the corner—we dropped in for coffee. It was normal to drop in unannounced for coffee an'. We talked about nothing in particular on the porches, on the corner, over coffee an'. It was just the pleasure of the back and forth. The banter. Not about the big thing we shared. Because we all knew what we shared. It was the sound and rhythm of the voices. The quips and the laughs and who died—who has terminal you know what—my teeth are giving me trouble—my piles—my kidney stones—my sugar. Those Rutger Place rich people talked the same way, just happy to hear one another's voices. Just like those old-time Rutger Place people, we were connected in East Utica to something larger than ourselves."

"People have to stay in the neighborhood, Senz, and not move around like nomads in the Sahara if they want to drop in for coffee an'. We became modern. We're only our lonesome selves now. We're connected to nothing larger, in which we lose ourselves."

"You were a nomad, going off to California, but you came back. To re-root."

"Those big elms converging over Rutger and Mary fifty years ago, and the cultures they sheltered—*were*. *Gone*. The *end*."

"Togetherness in a place. A world in a place."

"Whatever."

"Stop with this negativity. You have planted a wonderful garden in your own backyard, have you not? I have a plan for Utica, but I need help. I must remain anonymous and trust only you. (Pause.) I'm going to purchase one thousand sapling elms, the Princeton Elm, which is ninety-five percent resistant to that damned disease. I'm going to hire a crew to plant and take care of them for five years, until they're safely established. The entire length of Rutger and Mary and the rest here and there throughout the East Side, which has the cultures now of the Bosnians and the Hispanics. They are the hope. The Princeton Elm grows three to six feet a year. It withstands harsh climates and bad soil. Twenty to twenty-five years from now—"

"When we're dead and—"

"One-hundred-foot elms canopy the East Side. A beginning. Can you see it?"

"And you need me for what?"

"Front the project for Anonymous so I can continue to steal the Devil's money, because if my right-wing audience ever finds out I'm behind what they would believe is a homosexual project, they flee in droves. Will you help?"

"Join your insanity?"

"Please."

"I have too much time on my hands."

"You'll do it?"

"What do I have to lose?"

"Yourself! Wouldn't you like to lose it?"

Raymona enters: "We screwed up? You ate nothing."

They don't respond.

She says, "I can take a hint," and leaves.

"What I truly want, El, they don't have it tonight."

"Mushroom stew, Senz?"

"That they have. The other mushroom stew."

"*Utica* mushroom stew? Dunking the bread in?"

"Did you have to spell it out and break my heart?"

Senzalma goes to the restroom. Geraldine doesn't move. She says, "You're staying here, Conte. Don't move whether you need to pee or not. His prostate's bad. I don't care if yours is."

Senzalma returns and says, "I'm not stupid, Eliot. You wish to arrange through my terrible Uncle Carlo for a contract on your ex and her husband because you think it'll get rid of the guilt and the grief, am I right? Vengeance for the kids?"

"You're no angel in Devil's disguise either—you *became* the Devil with those race-baiting editorials in the *Observer-Dispatch*."

"Necessary camouflage, so I can continue to steal with impunity from the Devil."

"Two bodyguards, Tony. A security system in that vast farmhouse on Smith Hill that would win bin Laden's admiration. The fifteen-foot electrified fence encircling the ten acres. The state-of-the-art studio and transmitter behind the house. The armored limo with bulletproof glass. You go nowhere. You see only me. We eat in this cramped office with bodyguards because you fear, for good reasons, that people want to harm you. Kill you. Senz, the Devil is the most isolated being ever invented by the great writers. That's his punishment for being the Devil. The Devil says, 'Myself am Hell.' "

"That's certainly true and very nicely put. Myself am Hell. Which I am, in all honesty. By the way, Eliot, you're not exactly Mr. Social. Are you in Hell?"

"I live with someone."

"Hope to God you're not giving Catherine hell."

"I'm giving her head."

Senzalma blushes.

Geraldine snorts.

"As your friend, I'm asking a favor. I need contact info for Carlo Senzalma."

"I'm no expert on friendship, Eliot, but I don't believe a friend asks his friend to do a favor because of the friendship. What you want indicates what Geraldine sensed from day one is true. You need assistance."

"He's mental, Mr. A. He's a nutter."

"Arrange a contract, Eliot? Let's say the awful words: Arrange premeditated double murder."

Eliot does not respond.

"Are you and Catherine happy?"

"We're going through something now, but yes."

"You're happy with Catherine, vice versa, but you wish to order murder?"

"If you won't help me to contact Carlo—"

"Who will not deal with a person he would call a civilian."

"Then I'll—"

"Who will think you're FBI undercover."

"Then I'll—"

"Who will arrange a meeting with you in a little restaurant in South Philly, where you'll be assassinated."

"Then I'll offer the job to Geraldine for 100 grand."

Geraldine, in subfreezing tone: "Half now, other half on completion?"

"Yes."

"Fifty thousand up front?"

"What I said."

"Give me the up front in Proctor Park tomorrow after dark, then I'll dispose of your body in the trunk of your car. Mr. A, end this relationship."

"Eliot, if you pursue this sickness you will dishonor your relationship with Catherine. You will destroy it."

Geraldine: "Conte?"

"Yes?"

"Go home and get laid."

"She moved out this evening."

"In this weather?"

"Yes."

"Do you know where she went?"

"Yes."

"Go there and get laid."

"My dear Eliot, you have love and you want to order murder. How shall we make sense of that?"

No response.

"Kill two people who were never charged?"

No response.

"Kill them both, cover the possibilities?"

One by one, with deliberation, Conte overturns all the plates. Then the carafe of water. At the door, quietly: "Vengeance on behalf of my children. Yes." Conte slams the door. The temperature has plunged to twenty-seven degrees. Puddles and slush frozen over hard.

Dragan Kovac says, "If you're going, I'm going in. It's unhealthy out here the way I'm dressed."

"Take shelter."

Conte on the way to the car in socks—slips, slides, crashes to the pavement, banging his nose bloody.

"Mr. Conte! Your shoes!"

From the pavement, wiping his nose on his sleeve: "What about them?"

"You forgot your shoes."

"Fuck 'em."

Dragan Kovac watches Conte pull away. Removes his surgical mask and tosses it into the dumpster. He's about to go in when a car pulls alongside. The driver rolls down the window. Operatic vocal music. The driver shouts over the music,

"Sir, may I ask you a question? Sorry to bother you." Dragan Kovac needs desperately to pee. Nevertheless, hugging himself against the knifing wind, he walks over to the driver, who turns up the volume.

Shoeless, with the caution and appearance of a bent-over old man, Conte is inching along the icy path near the steps leading to his front door when he slips and crashes onto the second step, hitting his head hard over the left eyebrow. He does not yell out in pain. Not even a moan, as he crawls up the remaining steps to the door. The bathroom mirror tells him who he is: an overmatched boxer in the late rounds of a losing fight. Blood-streaked face. Cut and swelling over his left eye. Matching cut and swelling at the right side of his nose. What shall it be? He'd heard the answer at his first AA meeting. The nuthouse, the cemetery, or jail?

CHAPTER 10

11:15 P.M.

Conte sits in the kitchen, pressing ice cubes wrapped in a cloth napkin to his wounded face, staring at a bowl of Frosted Flakes. Five minutes later, he gives up on the untouched cereal, the improvised icepack, and returns to the bathroom mirror. The bruises now deep purple—the swellings, like eggs—the cuts, still oozing. The face of a man who walks on ice in his socks because he doesn't care if he hurts himself. Maybe wants to. The face of a man for whom the nuthouse looms. Who scorns the God God God rhetoric of the AA twelve-step method. Who has never reached out to his sponsor, until now:

"Kyle?"

"Eliot?"

"Sorry. I meant to call Mark's cell."

"Mark just got summoned to the Center on an emergency. Not even a hug goodbye and pale as a ghost."

"Was that a car I just heard? Are you on the street, Kyle?"

"Yeah. Walking Handsome."

"Walk him in the backyard."

"Huh?"

"Why not walk him in the backyard?"

"Because he won't do anything in the backyard. What kind of question is that? Because he regards the backyard as an extension of his domestic space, which he never violates—unlike some people who pee in their backyards. Even crap. This is not Handsome. This has never been Handsome."

"I advise you to walk him in the back."

"You're *advising*?"

"Out of range, in the backyard."

"You on some wild drug?"

"Go to the back immediately."

"Mind telling me why you're talking like a lunatic?"

"They're shooting dogs, Kyle."

"You need to work out more."

"They're shooting dogs."

"A lot more."

"Dogs of my friends are getting gunned down in the street."

"Eliot."

"If I knew why, I'd know who, maybe."

"Come over and we'll talk."

"I know what you're thinking. I'm not crazy."

"We can talk."

"Tell Mark I need to see him in the morning. Was that another car?"

"I'll come over to Mary Street and bring Handsome. He'll calm you down."

"Tell Mark."

"I certainly will."

"Don't forget."

"I certainly won't."

"I'm depending on you, Kyle."

"Because he's your sponsor, and you're in some kind of deep shit. Is that it?"

"You're not supposed to know I'm in The Program."

"I understand, but I do."

"It was wrong of Mark to tell you."

"He didn't. Something he let slip."

"I need to talk to Mark first thing."

"In the meanwhile, consider having someone like Handsome in your life."

"Listen to me, goddamn it! Get off the street!"

"I'm going to step out on a limb, Eliot. Because I sense it sometimes at our workouts. The thing I saw in Mark, ten years ago, before he went into The Program, I see it in you. It nearly destroyed us. The rage, the resentment, the paranoid tendency. You and Catherine, are you in trouble?"

(Silence.)

"Eliot, you still there?"

He's not. Conte shuts down his cell. Turns off the ringer on his landline. Unplugs the clock radio in the bedroom. Takes three ibuprofen and a double dose of a sleeping medication. At 5:45 A.M., he stumbles, hungover, legs like lead, to the kitchen for a mug of coffee, black, much sugar, and three glazed doughnuts. Checks the bathroom mirror. Could it be worse? Takes a second mug, black, much sugar, to his desk, where the message light on the phone blinks 5: The first is from the kind and pretty bartender at The Gay Martini, his guardian angel!, who identifies herself as Nikki Ryan and says she needs "to redeem the rain check you gave me right away" because her boyfriend has threatened in an e-mail, which she's forwarding, to "break every bone in my body." The second from Catherine Cruz, who says, "Pick up, Eliot, please pick up if you can hear me." The third from Detective Don Belmonte, who says he'll need to talk with him in the morning "around 9:30." Expects full cooperation and promises "very serious consequences" should Conte not be forthcoming. The fourth from Anthony Senzalma, who tells him that he will admit himself in the morning to Saint Elizabeth's for "extreme exhaustion on the verge of a nervous breakdown," and "by now, you know why." The fifth, from Mark Martello, 5:04 A.M., who only says that he'll appear at Conte's front door at 7:00 A.M. on matters of grave importance to the both of them.

He forwards Nikki Ryan's e-mail to Angel Moreno and asks him to hack into her account and the ex-boyfriend's and to let him know what he finds of interest by no later than noon. E-mails Nikki, requests the ex-boyfriend's physical address, place of work, where he might be located this evening. Urges her to go to a relative's or a friend's for the rest of the day and guarantees that her problem will disappear by day's end. He's about to shower and change for Martello's arrival at 7:00, who instead knocks at 6:35.

The sight of Conte makes it nearly impossible for Martello to know how to begin. With the tragic news from the Center? Which has been, and will be, withheld from the public for as long as possible, but which he feels compelled to relate to Conte? Or with Kyle's disturbing report of Conte's phone call, now dramatically enhanced by the battered face, the bloodshot eyes, the bedhead hair spiked out in several directions, and the pajamas that look as if they'd been worn for too many nights. The sight of Conte gives him an excuse for keeping the news to himself, at least for a while, of what had happened at the Center—the event that had devastated Martello and will do the same to this wreck standing before him. Conte, looking across the threshold at Martello, senses something much more painful than a battered face. The elegant, ironic Mark Martello, always with a twinkle in his eye, where has he gone?

After three seconds of mutual shock and silence, Conte motions him in. Offers coffee. Martello refuses. At the kitchen table, Conte, "I called last night because I'm in an extreme place."

"Eliot. Your face."

Conte explains, Martello replies, "You wish to hurt yourself?"

Conte digs into his cuticles, drawing blood, a compulsion since his teenage years, "The end of my rope, Mark."

"Yes. You are. Reason I came so early, I'm due at the Center at 8:00 for a press conference. Network feed, Eliot. I'm asleep on my feet and afraid."

"You don't look good yourself, Mark."

"Never mind me. I don't know if I can help you. I don't know if you can help yourself. The prayer of Saint Francis that's always quoted at meetings? Read it, memorize it. Better to comfort than to be comforted. Think about it. It works in hopeless situations. Like yours—and mine."

"Can I make you some breakfast, Mark?"

"Good. That's the idea. Very good. Thanks, but no. Have you tried comforting others lately? I mean, aside from offering me breakfast?"

Conte thinks he's comforted Catherine, though usually

it's the other way around. For some reason, he doesn't think of his long nurturing relationship with Angel Moreno and Angel's parents. He replies, "Yes, I'm giving comfort to Nikki Ryan," and when Martello says, "Who?" Conte explains.

"Are you serious? Saint Francis is appalled. Do you really intend to do violence? Or you're just going to scare him verbally? Right? Tell me the latter."

"The verbal method doesn't work with men who physically abuse women."

"Therefore?"

"Therefore."

"And you called last night because—"

"Nikki Ryan is in trouble and I'm going to help her. Why do you speak of Saint Francis in the present tense as if he—"

"You called last night because *you* are in trouble. Kyle says you were talking crazy. Have you done violence in the past?"

"Yes."

(Pause.)

"This must end. You can't do it tonight for this girl's sake, or for anyone's sake. Ever. Advise her to see your friends in the police who—"

"When they get around to it, next year, they talk to the guy, who if he hasn't already damaged her will take it out on her. That's how law enforcement works."

"Vigilante justice? You've done that before?"

"Yes. But never to nice people."

"I can't help you—you need a priest, a shrink. Both. You pervert Saint Francis. Okay. Okay." (Pause.) "You once told me that the only one of the twelve steps that made any sense was step 9, which doesn't require you to say God, but requires you to make amends. But we have to take the steps in order. You can't just jump to step 9. You need full preparation, but maybe in your case—maybe we have to be unorthodox in order to save the drunk and those he does violence to. You're not afraid to take the full consequences of your past acts of violence? Responsibility for the well-being of those you've hurt? And make amends to these victims? Is that right?"

"I love the beautiful spirit of step 9, but I can't do it. Because I'm not willing to bring serious harm to myself. One of those I've hurt is anyway permanently beyond my amends."

"This person has passed away?"

"That's one way of putting it."

"Are you implying?"

"Yes."

"You killed somebody?"

"Not exactly."

"Not *exactly*?! Ask God to intervene even though you don't believe. Pray to God in the face of your atheism."

"I don't know how to pray."

"Nobody does. Trying is good enough."

"Trying is good enough, Mark? That true? Our Father who art not in heaven, hollow be thy name."

"Stop with the fucking wordplay, Eliot. Prayer is the failed, but sincere, attempt to pray."

"I'll fail sincerely to pray for you, Mark."

"You're good at wordplay, Eliot. It helps you get through. Sophisticated escape, that's all it is, but it won't help you or me when you hear what I must tell you now. Last night ... last night at the Center. Last night in the detention cell, Novak and Nadija Ivanovic—they were found dead. They'd neglected to take his belt. He hanged her from the bar across the window. Laid her body aside, then did himself. They were found when a cleaning lady—NO!"

Martello (5'10", 165) is sitting in his chair. But chair and Martello are suddenly, violently high up against the kitchen wall at 6'3", 220 Conte's eye level. Eye to eye. A few inches apart. Hold. Five seconds. Hold. Ten seconds. Conte takes a quick, giant step back. The chair crashes to the floor, snapping off its legs. Martello is still sitting in it. Martello does not attempt to rise. Conte goes down on all fours. Again eye to eye, speaking now in a tone that Mark has never before heard.

"Are you proud of yourself? Do not avert your eyes."

"No."

"Those people are not terrorists."

Martello drops his head.

"Do not drop your head."

Martello raises his head, "They were innocent. I know that now. They were pawns."

"Mark, do not use the past tense."

"I'm sorry. They are innocent. Forever innocent."

"Forever dead. Their son, Mirko, my best student, eloped with a Catholic girl because he thought his parents wouldn't approve. That's why he disappeared."

"Not a terrorist either."

"This new Imam. You have him too. Has he hanged himself yet?"

"I released him."

"So that he can hang himself at home?"

Martello does not respond.

"The shoe is on the other foot now."

Conte rises. Says, "I'm making you a cup of coffee."

"No, thank you."

"The shoe is on the other foot now. Did you kill Novak and Nadija Ivanovic?"

Martello cannot respond.

"Your turn to say 'not exactly.' "

"I am responsible for their deaths."

"How would you like your coffee?"

Mark does not respond.

"I'm talking to you."

"I don't really—black."

"Sugar?"

"No, thank you."

"One or two spoonsful?"

"Do you mind if I get up and sit at the table?"

"Who recommended that you sit on the floor?"

He sits at the table. Conte prowls the room during what follows:

"Eliot. If it is your intention—"

"I don't have intentions. I'm just talking. I'm suggesting that you haven't earned your coffee."

"Are you going to hurt me?"

"Life is hard, Mark."

"I want to tell you what I'm going to reveal at the news conference. Please let me tell you."

"I like good stories. Yours good?"

"I'll tell you facts. During the Bush administration, seven years ago, Kyle and I were living in a D.C. suburb. I was a promising young Republican at the Pentagon in a midlevel post. Kyle was a freelance personal trainer."

"I already know this. This is not a good story."

"But you don't know this. One of his trainees was this district's congressman and your Hamilton College classmate, Rick Kingwood, married, three children, family-values champion."

"With the hots for Kyle."

"How did you know?"

"Married, three kids, family-values champion. Did Kyle return his affection?"

"No."

"I can't imagine Kyle sleeping with that prick."

"You don't have to. We had dinner at his home fairly regularly. Kingwood in the final months of Bush uses his friendship with Vice President Cheney to get a center located here, a ridiculous idea, lampooned in the *Times*, but embraced by his party, which was still at the height of its fearmongering powers. The unprotected heartland of small-town America et cetera. He gets me appointed director and we move to Utica."

"He comes home weekends, as usual, to press the flesh of his constituents, and Kyle's in particular."

"When the Republicans took back the House, Kingwood becomes chair of the House Committee on Homeland Security. He makes it his agenda to investigate American Muslims as potential safe-house providers for terrorist sleeper cells. He believes in himself as the next junior senator from New York. Small-town America's savior. He will run for the Senate. Has ambitions beyond the Senate."

"I know all that, Mark. Better tell me something new. Quick."

"This: A few months ago he tells me he has a high-level

mole inside Janet Napolitano's staff, a holdover from the Bush years who's feeding him information that would embarrass the President, but never gives me details. The President is soft on Muslims. It's in his Kenyan blood et cetera. Then a month ago he tells me he may have something very big, which might make America take notice of me. Open up all kinds of opportunities in and out of government, if only I'm the guy who can connect the dots. Six days ago, he hits me with the new Imam and his connections with radical Imams in Yemen and London, and a date. The Ivanovic family is implicated."

"Sunday."

"Yes."

"Help me to understand, Mark. The President of the United States, who put Osama bin Laden a thousand feet under the Indian Ocean, who decimates Al Qaeda leadership daily with these drone strikes, along with a few pain-in-the-ass innocent bystanders, this President has placed at the top of the Department of Homeland Security someone who looks the other way on a domestic disaster in the making? You bought that?"

"No. Napolitano didn't know. Nobody knew. King-wood gives me the name of the mole. I check. She's in fact a member of Napolitano's inner circle. He gives me her cell. She asks me to give her the middle names and birth dates of Kingwood's children, as well as his mother's maiden name, all of which I knew because Kingwood told her she'd be getting a call from someone who claimed to be me and unless the caller could give her such information she mustn't divulge anything. After I'd satisfied her, she said, 'It's in your hands now. Do not fail our citizens. This cell is disabled after I hang up.' Why would I think she might deliberately be feeding me false information?"

"Or that your Republican benefactor—the darling of the Right who got you appointed director—was an Islamophobic criminal?"

"Yes, Eliot."

"You wanted to be a great American hero, Mark."

"Doesn't everybody, Eliot?"

"Small-town America saved by an openly gay patriot. A book deal, personal appearances, speeches in the high five figures. What a great fuckin' country this is!"

"Last night I did the digging I should have done long ago. This new Imam was not conspiring with radical Yemeni clerics. He was not in touch with hotbeds of radical Islam anywhere else. This is what I know. He is no jihadi. This also I'm sure of: Mirko Ivanovic, like his parents, is innocent. At 4:30 this morning I was finally put through on a conference call to Napolitano and the President's national security advisor."

"You want me to believe that?"

"From 3 until 4:15 this morning I was threatening to go public with this embarrassment."

Conte standing behind him. Hands on Martello's shoulders, close to his throat: "Novak and Nadija Ivanovic are embarrassments? Is that how you think of them? You bastard."

"Please, Eliot. Don't hurt me. I mean politically, to the administration. You understand Napolitano knew nothing. The President is therefore in the dark. Only Kingwood knows. On Saturday before it's supposed to go down, he will reveal to the major networks what's to happen on Sunday, but thanks to him—he'll not name his sources of intelligence—the plot is foiled and Obama is exposed as incompetent to protect the homeland, as Cheney has been saying all along. Everything Kingwood has been selling about terrorist sleeper cells will now be endorsed by the so-called liberal media."

"But the good Mark got to the truth and destroyed Kingwood's ambitions, but only after pressuring two innocent people to their death."

"They finally roust Napolitano. The call is arranged. Just before 5 A.M., I get another call from the President's chief political strategist. I'll be naming the Napolitano staffer and Kingwood. He'll be finished by midday. His agenda is dead, along with his Senate ambitions. He'll face criminal charges. The mole is already in custody."

"And you?"

"I announce my resignation at the press conference."

"That's obvious. How are they going to take care of *you*, Mark? How will they show their gratitude?"

"I don't have to answer that."

Conte sits. Says with surprising gentleness:

"The God you believe in will put you in Hell."

"I'm already there and grateful to Him for giving me your company, as we burn."

"The event at the mosque on Sunday—it's on?"

"If they want it."

"Maybe you can be the guest of honor, Mark."

Showered, dressed and looking his best, the face aside, he sits on the couch, Detective Don Belmonte on the desk chair. Big

Don asks about his face, Conte replies, "I don't feel like explaining anymore." Big Don says, "Good. I'm pressed for time. Hope to God this chair can handle my weight."

"Where's Catherine, Don? I assumed she'd be part of this conversation."

"She's up the ethical morass without a paddle. Conflict of interest, not to mention she put herself on leave. Not to mention she told you about the Chief's dog, which I told her not to."

"She asked you to determine the Chief's whereabouts when the shooting of his dog went down. Did you?"

(Pause.)

"Not at home at the time."

"Why does he want the shooting kept quiet?"

"He says it'll become a racial thing, black-on-black violence, what do you expect of those black people et cetera. It brings him into racial question as the Chief, that's his concern. Look. I came here to ask questions, not to be grilled. The thought that the Chief did this, as well as the dog in Troy, is unworthy of an intelligent person who"—gestures at the walls—"reads all these books, but who maybe is not attached to the real world. I don't have all day, Eliot. That shell casing found at the scene of the Barbone murder matches one found at the Troy dog killing. As you must already know, thanks to my beautiful, indiscreet partner."

"Would you like a cappuccino, Don?"

"Forget the niceties. That stuff goes right through me, it takes no prisoners. There are tremendous things swirling, and you are the eye of the hurricane. Where and how did you get that shell casing?"

"At the scene of the crime. It was given to me."

"By who? Certainly not by lead Detective Mendoza, who by the way I intend to put in possession of the casing. Look, Eliot, Mendoza I can't stand, but this is beyond personal. One of the responding uniforms is my thought. Cazzamano, no freakin' doubt."

"Irrelevant, Don. You were given it. You intend to pass it on."

"Irrelevant? Oh, yeah?"

"Possibly it was given to me by the first civilian on the scene, who put in the call. A total stranger."

"I'll tell you why it matters. Sometimes these criminals who do these things can't keep away from the crime scene investigation. They're like freakin' playwrights at the premiere watching the audience. They get off on the spectacle they created. I've encountered this."

"Where, Don? On television? The movies?"

"If your father wasn't my kindest friend and supporter, I'd take you in right now for obstruction of justice."

"Don—"

"That loose cannon Cazzamano, right? He should go down for this."

Conte says nothing.

"You were at the scene of the Barbone murder, Mohawk at South. True or false, Eliot?"

"True."

"You were at Joey's last night, Mohawk at Lansing, just a few blocks from the Barbone scene, eating dinner with Anthony Senzalma. True or false?"

"True."

"You left by way of the back door of the office at around 9:45. True or false?"

"True."

"You left in a rage without your shoes. True or false?"

"True."

"You encountered Senzalma's bodyguard on the way out, one" (checking notes) "Dragan Kovac. Yeah?"

"Yeah."

"See anything in the parking lot of interest, like a car with its lights on maybe?"

"I have no memory of that. Why all these questions about my dinner with Senzalma?"

"Your anger blinded you to your environment? Have conversation with Kovac?"

"He complained about standing out in the cold. I told him to go in. That was it."

"This Rintrona and his wife. The Chief and his wife. All friends of yours?"

"Obviously."

"Don't get bitchy. Senzalma is a friend of yours, not so obviously."

"He's a friend. Which is nobody's business."

"You eat regularly in a hidden fashion with Senzalma in Joey's office?"

"Yes. The direction of your questions—"

"This chair is making a sound which gives me freakin' anxiety." (He gets up.) "I should take off a few."

"You're big, Don, but you carry it beautifully."

"Don't try to get on my good side."

"There's plenty of room on the couch."

"With my knees? I sink, I'll never come out. On second thought, give me the cappuccino because what's the difference at my stage of life?"

Conte in the kitchen attending to the coffee, Belmonte walking along the bookcases, reading the titles. He says, "I'm developing a theory about all of it. I'll tell it with the coffee and then I have to run. This Melville, you have a lot of his stuff."

Conte from the kitchen, "You know him?"

"I heard of him, but we never met."

Conte and Belmonte standing in the front room, sipping their coffee, swaying a little on the balls of their feet.

"I'm going to tell you something, Eliot, that hasn't been released to the public. In return, you're going to answer one big question and I don't mean who gave you the casing because it's irrelevant, maybe, as you say. When the coroner removed Barbone's clothes he found that his dick was cut off along with his balls. Nowhere to be found on the scene. The implications stagger me. Okay. So we got whoever killed your friend's dog in Troy and whoever shot Freddy in the head and cut off his equipment as the same person ninety-nine point nine percent sure. Then we have whoever blew away the Chief's dog and injured his wife, who we connect to the Troy dog and thanks to the casing also to Freddy's murder. What is the likelihood we have two dog killers on the loose? Those three killings are done by the same person. You agree?"

"Hard to disagree."

"You agree whoever shot your friend in Troy and then your friend's dog the next day is most likely the same person?"

"Definitely."

"So far everything, the two dogs, Freddy, and Rintrona, it's connected to the same person?"

"Makes sense, but far-out alternative scenarios could be imagined."

"The theory works even with last night's killing."

"What?! Who?"

"Dragan Kovac, maybe a minute or so after you pulled away in your socks."

Conte cannot respond. He sips his coffee. Once, twice, thrice.

"Not just any kind of shooting, either. Shotgun. One in the chest, which is unsurvivable, according to the coroner's preliminary report, and one in the face, which obliterates the face. What a mess, you wouldn't believe. Close range. Very close. You knew the guy well?"

"Whenever Senzalma and I—whenever, Jesus Christ, whenever we got together at Joey's, he's the first layer of security at the back door. He frisks me. A sweet lunk of a guy. Like a big child. Jesus Christ, Don, I can't take this."

(Conte sinks into the couch. Belmonte continues to stand.)

"I'm sorry, Eliot, but I'm running out of time. Two dogs and two humans killed and an attempt on another human, your pal Rintrona. Five events in three days. Someone is bingeing. Where does it end? I have a lot of work ahead of me. They threw me the Kovac killing. My theory says it's the same guy who did Freddy and everything else. Including Kovac."

"Why?"

"The unnecessary viciousness of the attack. Freddy's dead. He virtually decapitates him and cuts off his dick. Freddy's dick is nowhere to be found. Did the killer eat it? Kovac is dead, point-blank blast, he blasts again, point-blank, with a shotgun in order to make maximum ugliness of the body."

"Motive, Don?"

"Who cares? We have a pattern."

"That links maybe a perverted killer, you're telling me, to the rest? What possible—"

"Forget motive. Give me a latent print on the shell casing, we got the guy. The real question, now, is what do sexual mutilation and dog killing have to do with the attempt on Rintrona's life? Rintrona, your pal, why was he first? Every one of these events is in proximity to you. *You*. Even Freddy, who Mendoza went through his receipts from the day of his death and found your credit card had been run for a bottle of Johnnie Walker Black. You are somehow at the center."

"I'm having trouble accepting that part of the theory."

"Who the heck would want to be at the center of this sickness? Here's my question, which I don't expect you to answer now, but eventually. Soon. Rintrona was first. That's the key. Your friend. What is it that links you to Rintrona that triggers everything? I'll be back for another cappuccino and the answer. You have forty-eight hours, until Saturday noon, then I arrest you for obstruction of justice because of the casing. Can I say what a shame you and Catherine are separated? Your face says it all. You look lousy, Eliot."

He goes.

Conte knows the answer to Belmonte's question. He begins to imagine the far-out scenario, whose author is Antonio Robinson.

CHAPTER 11

Under the dead light of an overcast sky—forty degrees with a steady north wind slicing through his leather jacket—hatless Conte trods carelessly over icy sidewalks. Twelve minutes later, he knocks. The door opens, Catherine Cruz throws her hands to her face. Speechless, she embraces him while he explains—thinking, Is this man beyond help? He says, "Let's change the subject."

He enters, inhaling with pleasure. Walks about the apartment. Says, "Nice. New paint job." She tells him that Tom Castellano had every inch of every wall, ceiling, and woodwork repainted last year, and again a few days ago, even though the apartment lay tenantless all the while.

"When I signed the lease"—she as eager as he for distraction—"Tom said the odors of the past in here were stubborn ghosts that sucked his blood, and they'd suck mine too. He said he repainted for both our sakes. Tom said people should repaint their houses in and out, especially in, at least once a year—because who wants to live with the memories of themselves?"

"Amen."

"I don't, Tom said, do you. Then Tom added, I hope to Christ you and Eliot are not permanently on the outs. Is he as unhappy, El, as he sounds?"

"Tom's the happy philosopher of gloom."

"Are you as unhappy as you look?"

"Off topic."

"What's the topic?"

"Paint."

"Are we as unhappy as we look?"

He doesn't respond. Sits on the couch. She sits on the chair opposite.

"Say something, El."

"Why are you sitting over there?"

"You know why."

"We permanently on the outs, Catherine?"

"Permanently is death."

"Come home."

"Eventually I'll—"

"When?"

"One day at a time."

"For how many days?"

She says nothing.

"I can't repaint my mind, Catherine."

She comes over and sits beside him. Takes his hand.

"Don has a theory, Catherine. About all of the shootings."

"I know. He laid it on me last night, but not before asking if you owned a shotgun."

"No stone unturned. You see why it's a correct theory, don't you? The shooter could easily have gotten me, but chose instead to murder Dragan Kovac."

"It's only a theory, El. High-level bullshit. We need facts."

"You could be a target."

"And Tom? His German shepherd?"

"Yes."

"Shall we gather all our friends and their dogs and the kid next door, Angel, and take them to Fort Knox?" (She smiles a small, unhappy smile.)

"Yes, Catherine. Everybody to Fort Knox. You might be on a serial killer's list."

"Could be. Might be. Where are the hard facts that we need to stop this thing? Here's one: Don learned that Antonio was not at home when the shooting of his dog and wounding of Millicent went down."

"Don told me this morning."

"What shall we conclude from this? Nothing. It's just a lonely fact. Hard fact number 2: Don got the results from the tests done in Syracuse on the two weapons in UPD storage that we conclusively link to Troy. No evidence those guns were recently fired. This is definitive. But the technician noticed something interesting. The guns were immaculately clean in and out. No residues. No prints. *Redolent*, was the word she used, of solvents and oil. Not to be expected from guns that'd been lying in uncovered bins, in the UPD basement for three and four years respectively. The technician says no question these guns were very recently cleaned. Hard fact number 3: Don had our crime-scene forensics girl take a look at the Chief's driveway and adjacent lawn areas. She went with a flashlight and metal detector while Antonio was at the mayor's dinner last night. She was looking for the bullet. Or, more likely, its fragments."

"Let me guess, Catherine. She found nothing and Don concludes Antonio scooped up the evidence. Antonio goes to the mayor's dinner with Millicent in the hospital? Is that right? On the day she's shot?"

"Correct on both counts. These three hard facts are three unimpeachable witnesses on the same page."

"Don told me this morning it's crazy to conclude Antonio's our man. I think it's crazy too—and I think it isn't."

"Don's a pro, Eliot. He thinks all private eyes are amateurs at best and loose cannons at worst. He was holding out on you."

"Think I'm a loose cannon, Catherine?"

"Don't you?" (Her voice cracking. Steeling herself.)

(Pause.)

"So he doesn't let me in on the constellation of hard facts, but tells you, not expecting you'd pass it on?"

"He told you half of his theory, El. The other half is Antonio plus an accomplice."

"This is very high-level bullshit."

"When we're desperate, even bullshit—he doesn't think Antonio could have done it all. Don surmises that Antonio was the designer, but actually never himself—"

"Where's the motive for all this violence? I know, I know. Forget motive, find the pattern of facts. Bobby Rintrona, I can see it, and so can you. But the rest?"

"When we're desperate—"

He lays his head in her lap. She, who needs stroking, strokes his hair.

"So now you've betrayed the confidence of your partner by telling me the other half of his theory, and this is how we're intimate these days. But I don't buy it. Antonio's no psycho architect, though at this point it looks bad. Let's meet at Toma's for late lunch. Say yes."

"Yes."

"One o'clock at Toma's."

"Got it."

Conte at the door.

"You just got here. What's the hurry?"

Her question pleases him. Thinks it means that "eventually" won't be all that long.

He says, "I need to visit Anthony Senzalma at Saint Elizabeth's. He's had some sort of breakdown in the wake of last night."

"Millicent is there too."

"I'll see them both."

At Saint Elizabeth's: The door to Senzalma's private room is closed. Seated alongside, her weapon concealed, Geraldine Williams in designer jeans and a sky-blue blazer. As he approaches she stands, "He'll be happy to know you came when I inform him, but forget about going in, Mr. Conte. They gave him something special at breakfast. Twenty minutes ago I asked him how he felt. He points to the monitor and says, 'I saw myself on television eating ice cream.' "

"Give him my best."

"Yes."

"Geraldine—"

"Yes."

"I assume you were both questioned last night by Detective Belmonte."

"Yes."

"Did Anthony give him anything of interest?"

"He gave nonstop weeping."

"How about you, Geraldine? What can you tell me?"

"I saw nothing. I heard very loud music, thanks to you."

"To me?"

"You left the door ajar when you exited with your panties in a bunch."

"What kind of music?"

"People who like it call it classical."

"Orchestral or vocal?"

"Vocal, if you call a man screaming 'music.' "

"Anything else?"

"No."

"If you think of anything—"

"I won't."

"Tell Anthony to call me when—"

"He will. You're all he's got."

"You lost a colleague. I'm sorry."

"Yes."

"He was a sweet guy."

"Was."

"Uh, the music—fast or slow?"

"Fast. Depart, Mr. Conte."

The door to Millicent Robinson's room is open. She's in bed, sitting up, head tilted back, staring at the ceiling. He knocks.

"Look who's here—oh, dear Eliot! Whatever happened to you?"

"It's nothing. I fell."

"You expect me to believe that?"

He takes her hand, kisses her tenderly on the cheek: "Believe that."

"Do that many more times, Eliot. Slowly."

He blushes.

"Relax, hon'. I don't have anything naughty in mind. At this time. Now tell me the truth about what—"

"Milly, this is the truth—if I wasn't already madly in love, and if you weren't married to my best friend, I'd sweep you right off your feet."

"True lust, Eliot Conte, jumps over all obstacles. With ease. Your physique is lookin' mighty fine with all that working out you do."

He sits on the side of the bed.

"Shall I lock the door, Milly? Shall we practice before the main event?"

"I don't need practice, Eliot Conte, do you?"

He laughs. The grin lends a more horrifying aspect to his battered face.

She fixes him with a hard look. All playfulness gone. She says, "We've been seeing less and less of you for some time. How come?"

"We need to get back to old times, Milly. I've missed you both."

Can two dear friends, virtual brothers from childhood, possibly bear one another's company, one another's sight, after collaborating in murder of the first degree?

"What's the prognosis?"

"Knee replacement. After the holidays."

"In a lot of pain?"

"Not after what they gave me."

"Hard to believe what happened. The dog. You by accident. Who would do such a sick thing? Good thing Robby was at home."

"Who told you that? Who told you he was at home?"

"He's off Wednesday afternoons."

"He wasn't at home at the time. I had to crawl into the house and call him. He answered a half hour later. Know where he was? Bowling by himself, he claimed. Know what he was doing? Putting a heavy hard thing in the pocket. A strike in the pocket."

"That how he refers to bowling?"

"No, Eliot Conte, that is how I refer to fucking. He's been having an affair for the last two years, which is why he doesn't put a hard thing in my pocket."

Blushing, looking away: "Are you certain?"

"Does the Pope masturbate?"

"I'm stunned. You sure?"

"Like I said."

He looks away.

"This—Jesus, Milly. Sorry, I have a one o'clock appointment—I need to leave soon. What I want you to know, just between us, I'm pursuing an investigation of the shooting. Do you have any idea—"

"Some crazy-ass white teenage male with a gun having him some fun at this nigger lady's expense."

"I have a big favor to ask, Milly: Please don't tell Robby I paid you a visit."

"Don't worry. He wouldn't be jealous because he's having fun with his big, black gun."

"Think of it this way. He's got a private thing going, which we're supposedly in the dark about. Especially you. We also have a private thing going—let's keep it that way."

"What private thing do we have, Eliot? We haven't done anything. Yet." She laughs a naughty laugh.

Conte's in a bind. Robby must not know that he knows Robby lied about Milly being in Florida. He thinks it through: 1) She's angry at her philandering husband. 2) She's vulnerable. 3) She wants revenge. 4) He takes her (therefore) in his arms and kisses her deep on the mouth.

"Yet, Milly. We haven't done anything *yet*."

Kisses her deep again and leaves her, breathless and beautiful.

In the car, in the hospital parking lot, Conte checks e-mail on his iPhone. Nikki Ryan and Angel Moreno have responded. She gives him the address, in Utica's formerly exclusive, Waspy suburb of New Hartford, of Jonathan Figgins, owner of The Gay Martini, who appears nightly near closing time, 1:50 A.M. sharp, carrying a handgun, to collect cash and credit card receipts. Drives silver Audi A8. Sandy colored hair, 5'8", slim. Will spend night at her parents', North Utica, 424 Sunlit Terrace. "Jonathan is not especially fit. Thought you'd like to know."

To: Eliot Conte, Esquire
Re: Romantic Violence

Pursuant to request of 19 December, 5:47 A.M., we have determined that e-mail exchanges between one Jonathan Figgins (hereinafter Figgins) and one Nikki Ryan (hereinafter Ryan) reveal periodic tensions of ugly tone. We adjudicate in favor of Ryan, having determined Figgins is beset by jealousy re Ryan's commitment of affection. In latest iteration of said jealousy, Ryan is threatened for performing normal duties in position as female bartender of (apparently) considerable charm. Professional courtesy (strictly professional, she asserts) re customer of older male gender (one Eliot Conte) exhibiting alcoholic tendency. Said courtesy having been recounted (unwisely, we conclude) to Figgins in intimate setting wherein Figgins responded "break every bone," etc. Six months prior to "break every bone," etc. Ryan suffered fractured wrist (left) at hands of Figgins. We conclude, in regret, that Figgins's threat "to break," etc. must be taken seriously.

Ever at your service,
Angel Moreno

P.S. JEFE!

CHAPTER 12

Mohawk at South—Freddy Barbone shot and virtually decapitated in his liquor store, genitals severed and absent. Mohawk at Lansing—Dragan Kovac shotgunned behind Joey's Restaurant at point-blank range—once in the chest, once in the face. Mohawk at Eagle—Toma's Lebanese Deli and Mini Mart. In a display case up front, kibbeh, tabouli, stuffed grape leaves. At the other end of the store, several wobbly tables draped with plastic red-and-white checkered cloths. In between, four cramped aisles of sundries, beer, wine, energy bars, cigarettes, gum, detergents, bottled water.

What pleases Conte about Toma's is its seamlessly drab appearance. The weak lighting. The crowded space. A ceiling that would give some but not a great deal of clearance to a professional basketball player. The smell of coffee, too long roasted. Toma's—a token of the East Utica that was, where he discovered two months ago that it was possible, however briefly, to lay by his troubles.

He arrives under a still-leaden sky at 1:00 for his lunch date with Catherine Cruz, who's always punctual, but whose car is nowhere to be seen in the small parking lot. (Where is she?) He purchases two lottery tickets, as he does weekly, both for Angel Moreno, who says, weekly, that he'll "consider, but not promise, Jefe," to split the proceeds 50/50. Conte hears his name called out from one of the larger tables, squeezed into the far end of the store, where six hearty men, late seventies, hold forth on a regular basis. They know him as the sad-eyed son of legendary political boss Silvio Conte, a man for whom their respect was boundless, and so they were happy to invite him, ever since his discovery of Toma's two months back, to join them for breakfast on Tuesdays at 9:00 and lunch on Thursdays at 1:00, "because you have too much clogging up your mind, kid, and we're just the laxative you need." ("Kid," always, to Conte, at fifty-six.)

When the sight of his black-and-blue swellings draws no comment from the Gang of Six—no double takes, no stares, no looks of shock and concern—he's seized by self-consciousness. The Unimpeachable Remo says, "We've all been there, kid," Don gives the thumbs-up sign, Frankie says, "That's life, that's what it's all about," Gene says "Amen," and Conte's self-consciousness is suddenly banished. Remo urges him to join them, their treat, "because today, in this town, your money's no good," and Conte feels himself pulled pleasurably into the cheerful ambience of men who lament without letup, while having the time of their lives detailing a long list of bodily woes. They endure the surgeries, they endure the multiple daily medications and their side effects, they endure the restricted diets, they endure the insulin injections self-administered, "like junkies." Why? In order to "hang on," as one of them put it the first time Conte'd taken breakfast with the group, "as long as possible in this vale of fuckin' tears."

He regrets to inform them he has a date at 1:00 with an important person, he'll take a rain check, and sits at a table for two, five feet away. (Why is she late?) Paulie says,

"An important person. I get it. Eye candy for us impending corpses." The guys adjust their chairs so that he may partake of the conversation whose focus has been the two murders, the murder-suicide at the Oneida County Homeland Security Center, Mark Martello's sensational press conference, Janet Napolitano's statement from D.C. in which she praises Martello's patriotism for blowing the whistle on that phony prick Rick Kingwood, now in FBI custody. This spate of terrible news utterly delights the Gang which to a man recalls the Utica of their youth, featured in *New York Times* headlines, more than once, as the "Sin City of the East"—Utica, formerly home to two major Mafia figures, the Barbone brothers, Frank and Salvatore—seven very profitable houses of prostitution (in a city of a hundred thousand)—a high-stakes poker game that drew gamblers from all over the state and southern New England—and the site, over a thirty-year span, of forty-one unsolved gangland-style murders thought to be the work of Frank and Salvatore Barbone. "Professor Conte," Gene says, "Utica rises again. We're back."

The political, however, stands no chance against the personal: "Gene! My worthless prostate!" "Your prostate, Frankie? I bleed daily from below!" "Ever have floaters, Remo? I got floaters galore. I thought I was seeing little black bugs constantly right in front of my face. You know what my cold-hearted wife says, who shows me no fuckin' mercy for decades? She goes, You're drinking too much, Ray. You got those dts. My young doctor, who doesn't face what we at this table face at our point in the fuckin' journey of life, he goes, 'Why worry? It's natural at a certain age for the eyes to malfunction.' " "Gene, Gene, a fuckin' egg! Gene, a single fuckin' egg without salt and pepper! That's all I can eat without suffering"—says Billy, as he chews on his third baklava. "You know what I think to myself, Gene, more and more, lately?" "Johnnie, how on God's good fuckin' earth can Gene know if you only think it to yourself?" "I think, what's the point of going on? Why not take the fuckin' gas pipe and be done with it?" "What's the point? Is that what you're asking? The point, Johnnie, is you don't give them the satisfaction of watching you throw in the towel. That's the only point at our stage." "Give who the satisfaction, Gene? Who?" "What, Johnnie? All of a sudden you're naive about your closest relatives?" Belly laughs all around, especially Johnnie, including Eliot.

"So, Eliot, I seem to recall you knew this *disgraziata* Kingwood when you two were at Hamilton College." "I did." "What was he like back then?" "The same as he's always been." "A smooth, smiling, rich, condescending, my-shit-doesn't-stink scumbag, with beautiful manners?" "Too kind by half, Don," Eliot responds, "too kind by half." Don turns to Gene, "Too kind by half. Don't you just love this kid? Too kind by half."

1:18, still no Catherine Cruz. Conte excuses himself. Goes to the parking lot. Calls. Automated message. Returns. "What's the trouble, kid?" "No trouble, Billy." "She'll show up, Professor." "How do you know I'm waiting for her?" "Because only a woman of that quality could make a man of your quality et cetera. When she arrives, we'll all feel better in our decrepitude gazing upon this Latin knockout." "Eliot, this is what we do these days. We gaze, we fall secretly in love, and in the cold fuckin' silence of our homes, we dream." "Amen to that." Conte excuses himself again, goes to the parking lot.

Calls. She picks up, "Hey, sorry, on my way. Got tied up with the Wi-Fi installer who was late." "I got worried." "I know." "Real worried because—" "I know why. I'm sorry. See you in five." He returns, noticeably relaxed. Remo says, "Romantic anxieties resolved?"

Lunch is served to the Gang. The waitress, a recent Lebanese immigrant, asks Conte if he'd like to order. He replies that he's waiting for someone. The someone then comes through the entrance and down the aisle as the Gang starts in on the food. Remo spots her first, mumbles something, they all stand simultaneously as she approaches. Remo takes and kisses her hand. The Gang, showing impeccable courtesy, resumes eating—they quiet the cross talk, they respect, as best they can, the couple's privacy, five feet away.

She says, softly, "I have an update. The Troy detectives have canvassed Bobby's neighborhood three times for potential witnesses. They came up with nothing. They've reinterviewed Bobby and Maureen concerning the vehicles in question and report some progress. From Maureen, a white Ford, maybe, late model. She's mostly sure of white. From Bobby, a green Chevy, new, he's sure of it, with a partial plate I.D. Onondaga County, not Oneida as we originally thought. Probably Syracuse. Okay. Don has been coordinating with Tino Mendoza, but nothing there to report except this, and this is not small. Don kept the forensics on the Troy guns from Mendoza."

"He dislikes Mendoza that much he'll subvert his investigation? Wow." (Not so softly: Gene casts a glance.)

"No. Worse. Much worse. You know how close Robby is to Mendoza?"

"You're telling me he suspects Mendoza as the accomplice?" (Remo stops eating. Cocks his good ear in their direction.)

"He's not ruling it out. Here's the thing. Don has one of the department's secretaries checking with car-rental agencies in Onondaga County. If we get lucky—"

"Car-rental agencies in Syracuse? Because what killer in his right mind uses his own car? But, Catherine, Onondaga County is big."

"Patience and grunt work, El. That's always the ticket. This is not the movies."

"So we sit tight and hope he doesn't strike again?"

"Nothing else to do. We get the car, we get our man."

"This is what *I* have to do," passing her his iPhone with the e-mails from Nikki Ryan and Angel Moreno pulled up. She reads: "Are you telling me that you promised this girl that—"

"I owe her. I'm putting him out of commission."

At which point, one of the Gang, with passion, "McLAINE! THAT COCKSUCKER!" "Paulie, McLaine has been dead, what? Forty years?"

She says, "Who's McLaine?"

He smiles broadly, a Conte rarity, "Long story. I'll tell you sometime."

"El, you can't do this. We'll talk to her, gather the e-mails from Angel. Then I'll have him arrested."

"Out in twenty-four hours or less. You know this. Then what? She moves out of state in the middle of the night? Because he'll come after her. You know this as well as I do. That's what these abusers do."

"What do you propose, El? In order to put him out of commission?"

"I have a plan, short of putting him on a slab."

"Short of murder. Pleased to hear it."

"I'm going to take a hammer to his knees. I'm going to convert his knees to oatmeal."

(Frankie, whose hearing is almost normal, smiles and nods.)

She says, "We can't have this conversation here. Let's get something up front and take a ride."

As they rise, the Gang rises. Remo says to Eliot, "Kid, you need to spend more time here. A lot more." To Catherine, "Farewell, my heart."

Gene says, "Look who's here." At the display case, Michael Coca, in shoes that do not match, several days of beard, tapping rhythmically at his nose with a popsicle stick. Remo says, "Sad bastard. Walks all over town, even in this weather." Don replies, "He still drives, Remo. I see him once in a while in that '65 Mustang he keeps like new. He's nuts, but he can drive." "Remember my brother-in-law Tommy? In and out of the psycho ward for years before he took his life. He drove too. Let's be merciful." Behind Coca's back Conte steps out the door while Catherine picks up the falafels, the chips, two coffees to go.

She insists on driving. The overcast has partially lifted and the temperature fallen into the low thirties. She takes him up to the old lovers' lane, The Eagle, it's called by locals, overlooking the city on the high southern face of the valley, and parks alongside the huge iron eagle, perched atop its massive base. No lovers today, there for a quickie. Just Catherine and Eliot.

"Ever bring a girl up here, El, in your young manhood?"

"No."

"How come?"

"Didn't have a girl."

"The lovers who now frequent this place and the woods around here are lonely old men, who don't know each others' names. From all over the city, the county, and beyond. Lonely old men with wives, children, grandchildren. Eleven were arrested three weeks ago for performing sexual acts on themselves and others and for soliciting an officer in uniform. We kept it out of the Utica paper, but the pricks in Syracuse decided to run the story. Youngest sixty, oldest seventy-nine. Too old in a small town to come out, too late for liberation."

"Why are you telling me this?"

"I don't know. From up here in winter ... I don't know. The city looks sad. Listen. I want to tell you something. I've come to terms with what you and Robby did a year ago. Tomorrow I'm ending my leave of absence and going back to work with my partner. I can't justify what you did, but I can live with it. Some part of me even says you did the right thing. Now you want to do something horrific to this man Figgins on behalf of this damsel in distress who you barely know. That I can't live with."

"I didn't know the Mafia hitter, either, or his abused wife and child. Do you disapprove of what I did on the train to stop him?"

No response.

"Catherine?"

"Not completely."

"You partially approve? What does that mean? What can it possibly mean?"

"Have you done violent things I don't know about?"

"No."

"Eliot?"

"I said no."

"You intend to—"

"Yes. Because she's defenseless, and you know it."

"Something odd about her e-mail, El. She describes his slight physical size, with your imposing physique no doubt in mind, and tells you he's not that fit."

"Let's eat lunch."

"This is serious. You realize that she wants you to damage him?"

"I do and I will."

"You do and we're through."

"You mean that."

"I do."

"What can I do to change your mind?"

"Go to meetings regularly. At least once a week. For starters."

"What else?"

"Get therapy on a regular basis."

"What else?"

"Accompany me to 424 Sunlit Terrace, because we're going to have a talk with Nikki Ryan."

"Why? To what end?"

"I don't trust her."

"Shall we eat now, Catherine? Or shall we make love in lovers' lane?"

The overcast is blown out by a stiff north wind, the sky is pure, the city below is all ice and barren black boughs—the gleaming gold dome of the Utica Savings Bank brilliant in high relief. They set their box of food and coffee on the floor of the backseat. She straddles him.

After, he says, "We're not really through, are we, if I insist on my plan?"

"Yes, we are, and in spite of what we just did. Don't kid yourself."

Back at Toma's, one of the Gang of Six, seventy-five-year-old Billy Santoro, says, "I'm not right. I'm going home." He's offered a ride, but refuses, saying, "The exercise helps, especially mentally." Billy Santoro lives on Humbert Ave., a short two block street off Mohawk near South. He must cross Mohawk to reach Humbert and does so easily through brisk traffic. At seventy-five, Billy is still nimble. At Mohawk and Humbert he walks east to the second block of Humbert to reach his house, but must cross Humbert because on this day of dreams of Catherine Cruz, Billy had walked on the wrong side of his street.

Humbert Ave. is quiet on this Thursday afternoon. The street itself has been plowed and salted. Tire traction is perfect. No traffic, there rarely is much, no kids out playing, no strollers out for the bracing air. Billy steps out between two parked cars to reach his house, still dreaming of Catherine Cruz and hard of hearing, when a car parked twenty yards away pulls out. The driver floors the gas pedal, strikes Billy, and comes to a sudden halt. The driver looks in the rearview mirror. Sees

Billy, somehow not dead, raise his head. The driver backs up at full speed and runs him over, back and forth. Twice. There are no witnesses.

Mohawk and Humbert Ave.

In North Utica, where many East Side Italians and West Side Poles had moved on up, Eliot and Catherine turn left off Herkimer Road onto Sunlit Terrace, into a development built in the late fifties and early sixties, where working-class families who saved their pennies were able to purchase, for around $15,000, small but tasteful white bungalows with ample backyards and space along the sides ensuring privacy. The builder had generously planted two red maples in each of the front yards and now, fifty years later, full-grown and stately, they lend the street a look associated with upscale sections of town. The exteriors of the houses and the yards are fastidiously maintained, mostly by their proud second-generation owners who would not, unlike their immigrant parents, ever hear the epithet "dirty Wop" or "dumb Polack."

At 424, home of Nikki Ryan's parents, the two maples had been cut down and the stumps uprooted, three years ago, when the Ryans moved in, because Denis Ryan did not like the mess of fallen leaves in autumn.

Cruz and Conte at the front door, Denis Ryan answers in a short-sleeve golf shirt, fifth drink in hand. Cruz holds up her badge. Ryan wants to know who he is—Conte shows him his card—and what they want. Doesn't invite them in.

Cruz says, "We'd like to speak to your daughter, who we have reason to believe is here."

"She's not."

"Can you tell us, sir, where we might find her?"

"You gotta research warrant?"

"We're not here to search your house, sir."

Conte: "We're concerned about her well-being."

"She sure the hell is not."

Conte: "We're very concerned, Mr. Ryan."

"Where do Utica people like to go on their honeymoons, and you got your answer where she is."

Cruz: "She's gotten married?"

"Don't know if they tied the knot yet, but that's what they said."

Conte: "To whom?"

"Jonathan Figgins. He comes to the door. They talk in whispers so I can't hear. She cries. They embrace. She packs a suitcase. They go."

Cruz: "When?"

"About two hours ago."

Conte: "Are you aware, Mr. Ryan, that Figgins has abused her in the past and has recently threatened her with severe bodily harm?"

"She packs a suitcase. They go. This conversation is over unless you got some beef with me. Yeah, I'm aware he abuses her." Denis Ryan knocks back his drink.

On the way back to Toma's, where Conte will pick up his car, he's unable to speak. She respects his silence. In the parking lot she says, "El, you know what I know about people? I know nothing. How about you, El?"

He does not respond.

"But there are times," she says, "when I'm almost sure that I know you."

A blast of icy wind rocks the car.

He says, "Nikki Ryan. Who is she?"

She's turned to him. He stares ahead. Only ahead.

"I think you know, Eliot."

Something flits across his face: terror.

"She made a fool of me."

"No."

"I made a fool of myself. That your point?"

"No."

"Be blunt—I don't have time to dance."

"You're afraid, El."

"Of what?"

"How old do you suppose Nikki is?"

"Late twenties, early thirties."

"How old were your daughters?"

"Be brutal, Dr. Cruz."

"She's your fantasy daughter—at some level you know this. She's the fantasy who the heroic daddy swoops in at the last minute to save, who couldn't save his own daughters. Whoever she is, the real Nikki can't be saved. Your daughters are *dead*. I've never heard you say the word. Can you say it? You're alive on a half-time basis, dead the other half."

"My kids were doomed."

"You weren't there for them. Why? Because you made a choice. You want brutal?"

"Why spare me now when you never have before?"

"The cruel truth is that you have to find a way—by yourself, I can't help you on this—to accept some responsibility for what happened in California. You left your kids. That was your choice."

"I never chose to put them in danger."

"Unintended consequence of your decision to leave."

(Long silence.)

"I want to cry, but can't."

"It's a natural thing, El, a spontaneous thing to weep. You don't will it. Are you afraid to be sad? Hiding from your sadness in your rage? Stop hiding. Can you embrace the sadness? Dive down to the bottom of it? Then rise and find a path into the present, where we are? We're here. We're now."

"When we made love at The Eagle, that was my total present. At The Eagle, I was alive full-time."

"Me too. But now we have a serial killer at large. Nikki Ryan was a distraction from that too. Can you let her go?"

"My kids are dead."

CHAPTER 13

He's about to get out of the car when a text from Don Belmonte grabs her attention: "urgent be back on duty urgent mohawk humbert." No thought, not even a glimmer of a thought, precedes what Conte says, as the words tumble out of him with a will of their own: "There's something wrong with me."

Gesturing with cell, "I'm sorry—Don needs me now—I'm very sorry."

"I need you more."

"I'll come by after I"—gesturing with cell—"I have to deal with this."

"Why?"

"I'll come by later. Count on it."

He does not respond. Looks away.

"You can count on me, Eliot."

No response. Looking away.

Concealing her doubt, hand on his shoulder, "Look at me. We'll get through it. You'll change."

Looking away, "I've never changed."

"You'll see. Look at me. Please." (He doesn't.)

On the way home from Toma's, he stops at Hannaford's

Market and buys two six-packs of Excalibur, a nonalcoholic beer with the taste of poor-quality actual beer—tastes like piss, the saying goes—the label of which, in small print, lists among its ingredients a tiny percentage of alcohol. In the car out loud, with scorn, "I'm not having a drink," twisting off the cap, swigging deep, "just as Bill Clinton did not have sex with that woman." Finishes off the bottle, heads to Mary Street.

Home at midafternoon, pacing, half wanting to resist bottle #2, thinking he's as crazy in his own way as Michael Coca in his. What he did, in the snow, unforgivably, to that man. Only a crazy man. The contract that he wanted to put on his ex and her husband. Only a crazy man. Senzalma's words echo in his head, "You have love and you want to order murder?"

Denise's lovely face and form now vivid in his mind, what a big and blazing torch for Denise Coca he'd carried for several years before meeting Catherine. Did Michael know that Denise was drawn to him? Denise telling Milly Robinson, who told Antonio, who told him—who in Utica hadn't heard the sad rumors?—that she had decided to leave Michael after trying so hard not to. He'd been doing many strange things after his sudden retirement, a year ago, and his self-admission for six weeks to a psychiatric ward. Sleeping on the bedroom floor, moaning and rocking at meals, going on about the toxicity of Utica's water supply. She was putting up with it. She could take it—believed with all her heart until death do us part because she was a devout Catholic, but when she found him standing on the coffee table, giggling, pants down at his ankles, masturbating on the living room rug, she'd gone to see Father DeFazio, who told her that the Church would understand if she needed to leave him and that she'd not be denied the sacraments, or a request for annulment. "Michael is lost, Father," who replied, "But you are not."

Bottle #2. Down in one long swig. About to open #3 when it hits him—he knows suddenly against all reason—absurd to think what he thinks but is certain, nevertheless, that he's cracked the case. They would laugh him out of the D.A.'s office. Catherine would think he'd finally snapped beyond repair. They'd say, "You say 'somehow' this, 'somehow' that because you know nothing. Go home and work on your unreadable Melville manuscript."

Chops off several chunks from a one-pound block of hard provolone and eats them with stale crackers. Opens #3, but does not drink. Goes to his desk and begins to read the latest draft of his Melville manuscript. Smiles. Nods. He likes it. Forgetting himself for a while. Chops off several more chunks of provolone, puts them in his leather jacket, pours #3 down the sink. Leans over the sink and inhales the fumes. No buzz. Puts his .357 Magnum in his jacket. Who's next? Mark? Kyle? Their dog? Tom Castellano? His dog? Catherine, Angel, Angel's parents, Senzalma? (But not him, never him, and now he knows why.) How shall he convince them to be sufficiently frightened to—to do what, exactly? Lock themselves and their pets in their houses? And then? Leave town? Until?

Conte knocks at the Morenos'. Angel answers. Home alone. His parents are working late.

"Are you sure about that, Angel?"

"Your mind be leaving the good planet Earth, Jefe?"

"I wish to pay you for your work on Figgins and Ryan. You must accept this time."

"Nah, we straight."

"I'm afraid I need another favor."

"Don't be afraid, Jefe, because Angel already hacktivated Mirko and Delores in anticipation. Jefe, the love birds, they gone dark."

"Can you say where they might be? Might they be coming back to Utica?"

"Angel don't have spy machines circulating the third rock from the sun. Jefe?"

"Yes?"

"Can we assume you delivered rough justice to that motherfucker Figgins?"

"They got married."

"The female race, Jef, what can I say?"

"Keep the door locked until your parents return and tell them to lock it and not answer to strangers. This is the favor I need from you."

"When the fox returns, big man, all will be copafuckin-setic. You become like rational again."

Conte hands him six cellophane-wrapped chunks of provolone. "This is for you, Angel. Hope you like it."

"Kiss me, I'm Italian. Yeah."

"Yes, you are."

"Big man, Angel's got gourmet Mexican dessert."

(Conte hesitates at the threshold.)

"Jefe, I can't totally scarf it solo."

(Conte still at the threshold.)

"Jef, you be a total hound for sweets, it's like known up and down the Mohawk Valley."

Conte enters saying, "What gourmet Mexican treats do you offer, Angel, aside from your incomparable dialogue?"

"Chocolate chip cookies à la McDonald's, plus glazed doughnuts from the fuckin' Dunkin' franchise."

Through the short vestibule, gaily carpeted, they go—through the living room, to the kitchen where they sit, and Angel puts out the sweets and two cold glasses of milk.

"Full fat, Jef, because fuck the heart attacks, that other shit is tasteless."

"It is, Angel, but your parents, on the other hand, have exquisite taste, always have."

"Yeah, they like put in an order for the riveting presence they lacked in their humdrum lives prior to the coming of yours, in all sincerity, Angel Moreno."

"Angel, the gift from God."

"Yeah, man, I appeared from behind the burning bush."

"Actually, I was thinking of the tasteful interior decorating, you know? The furniture, such an elegant mix of contemporary and traditional, the colorful wall hangings and rugs, not to mention Florencio's artistic wall painting with those subtle pastels that define his taste—or should I say, his *sensibility*."

"Yeah, his *sensibility*, man."

"Not to mention the level of cleanliness."

"Man, my mother is totally anal."

"I admire your parents, Angel, always have. How are they doing?"

"I miss them, boss."

"You all live under the same roof. Children and parents together—that's the way it should be. Nothing better than that."

"Same roof, boss, that's only technical. My father works seven days a week and the little guy is exhausted 24/7. When he's home he's like falling into a stupor while eating, the food falls on his pants directly from his mouth. The little daddy is like here but not here and the mother not so bad, but bad enough. They come through the door, they don't have the energy to say hello. This is America, Jefe, the fuckin' Hispanic wave."

"They love you. That's always been obvious. They do their best, I know this. One love under one roof."

"Totally agree, but neverthefuckinless, Jefe."

"You want more of them."

"You said it."

(Silence, as Conte's mind flies thirty years back to California.)

"Jefe."

"Sorry."

"Where did you go, Jefe?"

"When you're older, I promise, I'll tell you."

"Jefe, you be like all of the sudden in the total dark."

"No, Angel, I'm in a place of light and goodness. Your house. And I'm thinking about your father and me planting the spring garden again."

"You into poetry shit?"

"You're a person of light and goodness for me, just wanted you to know."

"Going all wobbly on me, man?"

"Got a problem with that, little guy?"

"Nah. On occasion I dig the heartfelt thing. What I'm saying, I need *involvement* and propose you require help."

"Help?"

"Yeah. Don't think I don't know you're in hot pursuit of the maniac."

"How do—you've been into my e-mail?"

"Don't hold it against me, Uncle. I propose a team. Me Tonto, the cool Indian, you the Lone Stranger."

"Forget about it."

"You need help, Mr. C."

"You deaf?"

"But you do."

"So I'm told."

"Is that what the fox is sayin'?"

"No comment."

"Listen to the fox and take me on!"

"She wasn't referring to *that* type of help."

"Total head case type help?"

"No comment."

"Don't feel bad, Jefe. Angel is a whack job too."

"This thing is no joke. Listen. Get serious. It's dangerous, and I'm not letting you near it. Do you understand? End of discussion. Do you hear me? *Finito*."

"I'm here if you need me, Mr. C, including totally free psychological counselling."

Without another word they eat—all the cookies and all the doughnuts, gulping down the big cold glasses of milk in long, long drafts.

Back home, nothing to do, three hours since she said she'd come by, and beside himself and considering taking a dose of his sleeping meds to get through the hours until she—the phone, his landline. Caller I.D. CCruz.

"On my way."

"I'll throw some dinner together."

"Don't. I picked up Vietnamese."

She enters and first thing he says, "I have something important to tell you about the case."

"So do I. Let's eat first in peace."

They do. In silence. Wolfing it.

He says, "I'll do the dishes and then—"

"Let's cut to the chase."

"About the case I—"

"No. About what you have cold in the refrigerator."

"It's nonalcoholic. Nonalcoholic."

"Nice. A trace of alcohol is in it, as if you don't know what all drunks know. The gateway drink for people in The Program who can't embrace The Program. Like you. The slippery slope. For people like you who can't control their impulses. Who can't keep their shit together."

Conte opens and empties the remaining nine bottles into the sink.

"Did you do that, El, in order to please me?"

"No. And yes."

"Let's emphasize the no part."

"Michael Coca, Catherine."

"What about him?"

"He's our shooter."

"Oh, El."

She refills their glasses carefully to the brim with unsweetened iced tea. She says, "This pathetic man, whose insanity is on display in the stores and on the streets of East Utica, for the last year, whose wife has reported lunatic behavior in the privacy of their home, is none other than our killer of men and dogs. Why didn't I think of that?"

"If I was you listening to me, I'd be sarcastic too.

Remember Don's observation that all shootings occurred in *proximity* to me, as he put it? Close to the truth, but not close enough. All shootings *because* of me. Because I tortured Coca."

"You did *what*?"

"Antonio claimed that his assistant chief was a serial rapist on the loose."

"Michael Coca? A serial rapist?"

"Antonio was desperate to have me put him out of commission. He had no evidence, it was bullshit I quickly learned, but he wanted something extreme done to Coca. Because Coca was blackmailing him."

"About what? Are you telling me he wanted you to kill Coca?"

"No doubt. But we only extracted key information out of him."

"*We*? *Extracted*?"

"Bobby and I. We tortured him. In wild disguises. We were beyond recognition. Don't ask for details."

"Who have I been sleeping with for the last six months? You and Bobby did actual torture?"

"Strictly psychological."

"Strictly psychological? I'm supposed to find that comforting? And what else? Witty? You want me to applaud your wit?"

"It was Coca who coughed up Antonio's complicity in the triple Mafia hit. This was the subject of the blackmail. Coca wanted to be chief. After we were through with Michael, we brought the Mafia hitter to Antonio."

"Don told me when I came onto the force that Coca suffered a total breakdown. Don told me he's in a mental ward for six weeks about a year ago. Because you and Bobby? Don told me Coca retires from the force one month after the mental ward because you and Bobby? First you and Bobby are accomplices in murder."

"Yes."

"Now this."

"Yes."

"Coca's motive."

"Yes."

"Any more violent secrets you want to reveal? Are there more?"

"No."

"Are there *more*?"

"No."

She pushes back against her shock. She'll stay in the hunt.

"It's obvious, Catherine. Unlike you I don't trash thinking about motive. Now he's turned the tables and I'm the subject of torture. He wants me alive to suffer the suffering and deaths of those close to me. I'm to be spared for impotent suffering."

"Didn't you just tell me you and Bobby were disguised beyond recognition? Did either of you speak?"

"Just Bobby, whose voice he never before heard."

"How then could Coca possibly know it was you and Bobby?"

"Somehow he does."

"Somehow. Ladies and gentlemen of the jury, somehow."

"Legally my theory is without foundation. It's a joke. I understand that."

"Explain why Antonio didn't eliminate Coca too."

"No need to, a guy that far off the planet."

"You were not close to Freddy Barbone. How does he fit?"

"The shattered bottle of Johnnie Walker near Freddy's body. I think it was a message."

"An old pop tune. Remember? Dionne Warwick. A Message from Michael. Or was it a Message *to* Michael?"

"Make light of my thinking. Go ahead. But—"

"You're calling this *thinking*?"

"His public and private acts of madness are pure theater, Catherine. No, please, take me seriously for a moment. It's been a yearlong performance at home and on the streets guaranteed to place him far beyond the zone of suspicion. Who would ever believe he's the one?"

"Only you."

"He's insane by any measure—but lucidly insane—brilliantly insane. Don's latest theory that it's Antonio with Tino as agent of Antonio's intentions proves Don's over the hill. Ridiculous. Implausible."

"But less ridiculous and less implausible than yours."

The phone. Antonio on the answering machine: "You there, El? You listening like a fuckin' pervert? Guess who we got locked up for at least forty-eight hours? Our friend Michael Coca, who Cazzamano and Crouse arrested on Bleecker and Mohawk about an hour ago for indecent exposure. He grabs Cazzamano's crotch. He offers him a blow job, which knowing Victor's democratic appetites I'm surprised he didn't accept. Victor puts the club to him. Man, you and that Rintrona did a job on that son of a bitch. What can I say except fuckin' bravo. Speaking of sons of bitches, that call you made to me? You cunt." He hangs up.

"Theater, El? More theater?"

"The only question now is who's next? You? But not me. Never me. Who's next?"

"On your theory, with Coca behind bars, everybody's safe well into Saturday night."

He nods.

"El, this afternoon we had another murder."

"Who? Someone close to me. Yes?"

She has difficulty getting it out. "Billy Santoro."

"Something happened to Billy?"

"He was murdered."

"What are you trying to say? What do you mean, murdered?"

"Murdered. Deliberately hit by a car on Humbert Ave."

"I saw him today at Toma's. When we left he was still at Toma's. Am I wrong? Are you suggesting I'm wrong? What are you trying to say?"

"I went to the scene on Humbert Ave. after we parted. That was what the text from Don was about. The responding patrolmen thought it was a simple hit-and-run fatality. They were wrong. He was hit and then the driver backed up and ran over him backing up. Put it in drive and ran over him again. This is what the tire skids on either side of the body tell us. Initial hit—hard brake. Reverse. Hard brake. Forward. Billy's body, in all my time in Troy I never saw such a brutalization. Eliot?"

He's gotten up, back to her, hands on wall.

"Eliot?"

"I'm here."

He sits. Leans across the table, takes her hand—squeezing too hard.

"Billy wasn't complaining about his prostate today. He pronounces it 'prostrate.' "

"I've interviewed," pulls her hand away, "the guys, Gene, Remo, Don, Paul. They're shattered. They couldn't give any help. Paul said the last few days in Utica are like a horror movie. God help them. Gene said Billy wanted to walk home. It's not that far, after all. He usually walks to Toma's, then gets a ride home, usually from Remo."

"I gave him a ride once."

"I know how you feel about the guys at Toma's."

"I know how I feel."

"I want to talk to you about a pattern."

"A pattern of funerals. I need to be at Billy's wake. I need to be at the Ivanovic wake. Do Muslims have wakes? Kovac is from Cleveland. They'll ship him back to Cleveland. A closed casket for Dragan Kovac and a closed casket for Billy. His kids will put a framed eight by ten on top of the casket." (Pause.) "I just can't sit around. I can't be expected to sit on my hands. I need to do something."

(Softly:)

"I want to discuss a pattern, El."

"I want to discuss Michael Coca. He was at Toma's when we left. Have you forgotten?"

"El, I asked Don Ayoub if he noticed anything unusual when he left shortly after Billy did, and he said he saw Coca's vintage Mustang across the street in the Aroma Café parking lot. I asked him why he was telling me that. He said because it was unusual to see Coca's car anywhere. At the time, I thought nothing of Don's observation. Just an old friend of the victim trying to be helpful to the investigating detective."

"Please don't call Billy the victim."

"Maybe I'm willing to rethink my reaction to your theory. Rethink but not necessarily accept."

"He sat in that car, Catherine. He saw Billy start to walk home. He drove to Humbert Ave. and waited for Billy. This is how it went. Pick them off one by one who have proximity to me. To my list of the vulnerable we have to add all the guys at Toma's."

"Murder and brutalize the body. Barbone, Mohawk at South. Kovac, Mohawk at Lansing. Billy, Mohawk at Humbert Ave. Valley View Road where Milly's dog was shot and Milly wounded. Valley View Road is essentially an extension of Mohawk, is it not? A pattern of Mohawk, El, what does that tell us?"

"Mohawk is beside the point. The insult, the desecration of the bodies. That's the point."

"El, what is the point, exactly, of the desecration?"

"I don't know. Coca's point is irrelevant."

"Whoever it is—"

"It's Michael. Stop resisting me, Catherine."

"He's shrewd, whoever it is. He picks his times. When he won't be spotted by witnesses. Though Humbert Ave. at midday is risky."

"He's losing control."

"Will you lose control?"

He averts his eyes.

"Let's say it's Coca, El, because he wants revenge on you. Wants you to suffer a living death. Okay. How do we tie him *evidentially* to the killings?"

"If we can place him in the rental car—"

"That would be huge—"

"If we can show that he had access to gun storage at UPD—"

"Where does he get the keys, El?"

"He had them when he retired. He had them duplicated before he left the force."

"No locksmith—it's against the law, El, to duplicate those keys."

"Catherine, this is Utica."

"Why would he return the guns to storage?"

"To make sensible people like you and Don and me make stupid conclusions about Antonio. Which we did. What do we know now about Onondaga County car-rental agencies?"

"Nothing. One of our clerks went to work on it late this afternoon. She'll be back on it in the morning."

"You know damn well I'm right."

"We have nothing except your guilt and fear, but I half buy your idea."

"Stay here tonight."

"Okay."

"Shall we get some arctic air? Let's take a walk around the block."

"Let's do that, El."

As he takes his jacket off the coatrack his .357 slips out and clatters to the floor.

She says, "I don't think we need that for a walk around the block."

"We're taking a walk around the block—that's why we need it."

CHAPTER 14

She's back in his bed after a three-night absence and for the first time in years Conte sleeps the sleep of an innocent youth—nine unbroken hours. He awakes to find Catherine gone. A note on the kitchen table.

El—

Don texted at 8:00. Rental agencies refuse cooperation unless an officer with UPD credentials appears in person. The Chief nominates me. The list is long. If you don't hear from me, we're still up the creek without a paddle. Get some exercise. Talk to your paesan Melville.

Love, C

Get some exercise. Talk to your paesan Melville. Just a few ordinary, a few lighthearted words—that's all it takes to quell the rising anxiety about her absence. Catherine of Troy, as he likes to call her, is not—on this morning—among his troubles.

After his cappuccino and favorite toast—a slab of crusty Italian bread slathered with mango-ginger chutney—he calls Kyle Torvald to ask how he and Mark are holding up. Kyle tells him that Mark is in D.C.

"They're grateful, they're going to take care of him."

"You two moving back to D.C.?"

"Inside the Beltway, Eliot, politics—they eat it, they drink it, they defecate it, then they eat that. They slurp it up. He's moving back. I'm not."

"You're breaking up with Mark?"

"It'll be a commuting relationship, but I'm not commuting. Utica for me."

"You're really calling it quits?"

"I am, but Mark isn't. He'll come up every weekend. After awhile, every other. Then once a month. Eventually he'll realize there's no point. You missed your Wednesday workout. Want to make it up? I'm free at noon."

"I'll be there."

"Uh, Eliot, that call you made the other night? They're shooting dogs and their owners? Et cetera?"

"It's true."

"It's true?"

"Yes."

"Uh, Eliot, a lot of people in this town have dogs. Why me? Explain that."

"Because you're a friend of mine."

"Buddy, you need the cure, and I'm going to administer it."

"What's that, Kyle?"

"The Enhanced Suicide Stairs. Which I'll do with you in case you require mouth-to-mouth resuscitation. Will you accept, needs be, mouth-to-mouth from a nonflaming gay man? Noon."

"Seven flights?"

"No. To the top."

"Ten flights?"

"You heard me."

"I doubt I can handle that."

"Save your whining for Catherine."

After cappuccino #2, he switches to a double-shot espresso, thinking about all those double shots he used to spike with anisette—the anisette progressing, at his worst, to half the volume. Calls Antonio Robinson at the office:

"Robby."

"Don't Robby me."

"Listen—"

"You want something from me?"

"No. From us. Our friendship as it used to be."

"It's over. Think I don't know what you were implying on the phone call you made? Supposedly concerning Milly? You think I shot my dog and accidentally wounded my wife? You motherfucker."

"I don't think you were the shooter."

"When I told you she went to Florida for the fuckin' holidays? It was bullshit."

"I know."

"You knew when you called?"

"Yes."

"Bastard."

"Yes."

"You want information on our friend? Is that why you called?"

"What's his behavior like?"

"Why should I tell you?"

"Eventually I'll get to that."

"Get to it now or this conversation is over."

"He's done them all. He's the shooter."

"Including JFK?"

"In Troy and Utica. Including your dog. He's the shooter."

"Last night, at dinnertime, Molly Barnes, who brings the trays to assorted scumbags for twenty-three years, who takes communion every morning, when she gets to his cell she finds your shooter buck naked. He proposes marriage. He's nuts for a year at home, he's nuts all over town, he's nuts here."

"It's an act. Utica public theater."

"You don't sound like you've been drinking again."

"It's a diabolical cover."

"You're not slurring or have you just lost your mind like the naked man who wants to spend the rest of his life with Molly Barnes?"

"He's the one."

"You have evidence, brother asshole?"

"Nothing now that'll hold up, but I have confidence that Catherine—she's going to come back with a name, Robby. Because you obviously can't rent a car without showing a license and proof of insurance."

"She comes back with a name, sure, we're almost home."

"How long can you hold him?"

"Forty-eight hours. She doesn't come back with the goods, he's out tomorrow night."

"Six acts of violence in four days, Robby. Yesterday, Billy Santoro. You'll see nothing today and nothing tomorrow while he's still locked up. Mark my words."

"This maniac, let's say it's who you think, why does he

switch to first degree vehicular homicide? Tell me why. Tell me what you have that will stand up in court. Tell me something besides your finger up your ass."

"Revenge on me for what I did to him."

"So he kills my dog? Why didn't I think of that?"

"I can explain it all."

"Right now I have something major on my agenda."

"What's that?"

"My morning crap."

At noon, after two cappuccinos and three double shot espressos, Conte enters POWER UP! and hugs Kyle—he's not done that before—and Kyle responds, "Out of sympathy for my situation you've decided to come out of the closet? What happened to your face? The first time I saw you you'd just been taken apart by someone you know, but won't reveal. Who did it this time? Same guy?"

"I did it to myself."

"I don't know what to say, Eliot—except you scare me."

"It was an accident."

"What did you do to make Catherine so angry?"

"Come over tonight and I'll cook you a fine dinner. Bring the dog."

Kyle shakes his head, sadly, puts on his hard-ass personal trainer mask, orders Conte to the rower, five hundred meters, "but don't go all out, or you'll be sorry." After a few gentle stretching exercises, leads him to the airless interior stairwell where he says, "On second thought, for this challenge, I'm not going to join you. You need to face your fate alone."

The Suicide Stairs is a timed exercise consisting of running as fast as one can, two steps at a time, if one can manage that, to floor #7 (in past iterations), then down as fast as one can, to floor #1. Then back up to #6, then #5 et cetera. A somewhat merciful descending ladder—the hardest ascents coming at the beginning. "To assuage pussies," Kyle says.

"This time," Kyle smiles, "ten flights in ascending order, up to two, down, up to three, down, so forth because it pleases me to reserve the hardest ascents for the end. When you start up on the final ascent, ten, death speaks as you reach landing five, and I won't be there to distract you. At landing six, you welcome actual death alone. Ready? Wait. At each landing, five push-ups."

When he's done, he collapses at Kyle's feet, who says, "Twelve minutes, thirty-one seconds. Not bad for a paranoid pussy. What are you cooking tonight?"

"This is sick, that I pay for this."

"Here, at POWER UP!, Mr. Conte, we become sick in order to become well."

His workout over, he calls Rintrona, tells him he's coming down to Troy, "right now," and will meet him at the Melville Diner. Rintrona informs him that Loretta and Big Paulie sold the business to members of the Twitter generation, who've renamed the diner Café Troy. He hasn't brought a change of clothes to POWER UP! He could shower there, but he's in a hurry to see his wounded friend and give him the news of the breakthrough.

At a wrought-iron corner table with a glass top, Rintrona

sits beneath a luxuriant ficus. Conte says, "How are you feeling, Bobby?"

Rintrona answers, "What happened to your face?"

Conte says, "Your voice sounds almost normal. Feeling better?"

"Better? What I'm on for pain? No wonder they become addicts. What happened to your personal hygiene? What happened to your face?"

"Irrelevant. I have news you've been waiting for," and proceeds to tell him about the several events of Utica violence, the forensic link between the Troy and Utica weapons, his certainty that Michael Coca is the doer in all instances.

The waiter, tattooed, beringed, asks if they'd like to order, taking a step back from Conte's odiferous presence. Rintrona says, "What's a salad sandwich, kid?"

"Lettuce, tomato, cucumber, mayonnaise on wheat."

Rintrona says, "Guess what, son? I can read the menu description. But what the fuck *is* it?"

"An Irish import, sir."

"From the famine days?"

"Sir, there are other choices."

"I choose the famine special in honor of my Irish wife."

"Me too," says Conte.

"Something to drink?"

"Water."

"Bottled?"

"The tap free?"

"Yes."

"And you, sir?"

"Tap for me."

Rintrona says, "Your theory, my gut says you're right, which is why he came for me first. My gut says, let's take him off the street when he's out tomorrow night. My gut says, let's ensure he's had his last birthday. But as a law enforcement officer, I have to agree with Catherine and Robinson that you have nothing of legal significance. You want us to believe he played the role of a nut job for a whole fuckin' year in order to—no way, Eliot, because that idea is evidence that Eliot Conte has lost it. You've given me nothing. Consider psychological counseling."

"I promised Maureen I wouldn't tell you what she told me. The shooter who killed your dog, who killed Aida—"

"Don't say Aida's name."

"Maureen said he was playing operatic music at high volume when he drove up. See where I'm going with this?"

Rintrona stares, but does not respond.

"Maureen says she thought it was Verdi because this is what you mainly play. A lot of Verdi at home and in the car."

Rintrona says, "How long does it take to make a salad sandwich?"

"Maureen recalls nothing but a few notes, which she can't get out of her head." Eliot sings them, not softly enough. The cashier glances over.

"The last few days, Eliot, she's been going through my Verdi collection from his first opera through his middle period. I'm thinking something's screwy with my wife. Last night until two in the morning and this morning starting at seven it's the middle period. I'm worried. This is not Maureen who can take or leave opera. She's gone off her rocker, thanks to what happened to us. I told her this morning she should get away from it all. Go to her sister's in Minnesota. She says, 'Don't bother me, Bobby, I'm trying to concentrate.' Then she puts on—"

"Listen, Bobby, the shooter who did Dragan Kovac also blasted operatic music. We know this from a witness."

Rintrona rises, goes to the waiter, returns, muttering "Café my ass. 'We're working on it, sir.' Okay, Eliot. We blasted it when we tortured Coca. This is your evidence, right? Which no one in the legal arena—they'll lock you up in the fuckin' mental ward if you tell them this. We know, okay? *We* know. This morning, Maureen was concentrating on the final-act trios of the middle period. She starts this morning with *Luisa Miller*. I say to her, 'You know, Maureen, *Luisa Miller* is not considered middle Verdi. It's *Rigoletto*, *Trovatore*, *Traviata*.' She says, she completely shocks me, she says, '*Luisa Miller* is the transition, Robert, between early and middle.' She says, 'Verdi became himself as this opera progressed to its final scenes.' Eliot, I'm speechless. She says, 'You dragged me to a lot of operas, I have to listen to it at home constantly. You think I didn't absorb, Robert? I know more than you think, have a little respect for your wife's musical understanding.' When she calls me Robert, I fear my wife."

"What I'm thinking, Bobby, she's trying to identify what the shooter was playing. She thinks it'll help me in the investigation. But we know, don't we? We *already* know. He was no doubt playing the famous tenor number from *Trovatore*, which we played full blast when we did the job on Coca. The shooter is Coca. Can you doubt it?"

"Who shot me three times and murdered my dog. Miserable cocksucker."

"Yes."

"Who will never be brought to justice, Eliot."

"Unless Catherine puts him in the car you gave a solid I.D. to."

"If she does, we don't have to do what we have to do. She doesn't, we pick him up tomorrow night. You watch as I ice this miserable cocksucker."

"But we wait on Catherine's report because—"

"It's better to go the legal route? Bullshit. It's better if I do him privately—first I'll cut off his balls and make him eat them—then I'll—"

"She comes up empty, I'm with you all the way, Bobby. We do the job on him. Tomorrow night, she comes up empty, he's dead. And I won't be just watching, believe me."

"In the son-of-a-bitchin' meanwhile?"

"Tomorrow afternoon, you know what's playing at The Galaxy? Live from the Met? Anna Netrebko, Jonas Kaufmann, Erwin Schrott."

"*Trovatore*. The cast gives me a hard-on."

"The four of us at The Galaxy. You feeling well enough to do it?"

"For a smart guy, Eliot, you just asked me a stupid question."

The sandwiches arrive. Rintrona bends his fork in half, says, "I'm not hungry." Eliot puts a twenty on the table, eats his sandwich on the way out.

In the parking lot of Café Troy, Conte checks e-mail. Two messages:

Eliot, Nothing. Still up the creek without a paddle. Be home for dinner around six. —C

My dear Eliot,

Had I been kind and permitted Dragan to come in on such a bitter night, he would be alive. I fly to Cleveland soon to attend his wake and burial. I cannot forgive myself. Why should I be forgiven? I am, as you so wisely urged, at long last coming out of the left-wing closet and have communicated my decision to my producers who say that I have a contract, the lawyers and so forth.

My publisher has no problem and wishes to substantially add to my advance if I will write forthrightly about my secret life. After Cleveland, I will take a week at an undisclosed location, which I disclose to you alone. The Presidential suite at Hotel Utica. Geraldine returns to Phoenix on Monday. She tells me that before she leaves she wishes to say goodbye to you. She expressed fondness. I believe she has something on her mind other than your offer to pay 100 grand for you-know-what. I believe she's been nursing a crush on you. Geraldine Williams is a very serious person. Her name is not Geraldine Williams. If I told you her true name you would be shaking in your boots. Be very polite when you see her, be very sensible. Visit me, please, I beg you.

Love, Anthony.

Catherine and Eliot are walking to The Chesterfield for dinner. He tells her about his day. She asks how Rintrona is doing. He tells her, "Surprisingly well."

"I presume you gave him your theory?"

"I did. I told him that it would be better if Coca were arrested."

"Better? Better than what?"

"I meant that—"

"I know what you meant, Eliot."

He doesn't respond.

"Better than what? Answer me. Better than murdering him?"

CHAPTER 15

FRIDAY NIGHT, 10 P.M., CONTE'S BEDROOM

He's undressing—she is not. Takes her hand and tries to lead her to the bed. She resists.

She says, "You and Bobby talked about it, didn't you? Killing Coca."

"Bobby did."

"You did too, didn't you?"

"I put the lid on it. I have no desire to be a vigilante."

"Don't lie to me, Eliot. You're convinced, evidence or no evidence. We don't come up with hard evidence, real soon, you'll take him out."

He embraces her: "Let's finish what we started in the living room."

"Forget Coca. (Pushing away.) He did not rent a car in Syracuse. This is what I learned. Get it through your head: He did not. That partial plate Bobby gave us? Assuming it's accurate with him shot three times, on the ground, in the weak light of dawn? Refers to over eleven hundred vehicles privately owned in Onondaga County. See what we're up against? We have nothing but your feelings. In other words, we have nothing. Put your pants back on."

"Tomorrow is another day?" (Hand on her crotch.)

"Definitely. And yesterday, by the way, was the day before today."

At the front door, still in his briefs, still turned on, he asks how she acquired the list of rental agencies.

"Becky Altieri, the part-time assistant to Antonio's executive secretary, who e-mailed it to me."

"She got it via Google?"

"Of course."

"Still have it on your phone?"

"Naturally."

"Send it to me." (She does.)

"May I ask why?"

"I'll tell you when I know."

(She goes.)

SATURDAY, 7 A.M., UPD LOCKUP

Seventy-four-year-old Lydia Abraham, a thirty-year volunteer, approaches the cell holding Michael Coca to find him naked and on his knees in the prayer position of Islam.

She says, "Good morning, sweetheart. Got your oatmeal. Dear me, aren't you cold like that?"

He responds from the prostrate position, "Bring me a lawyer and a half cup of brown sugar."

Ten minutes later, a uniformed officer appears with a cell phone. Coca asks Information for the number of Utica's most legendary attorney, Salvador J. Capecelatro, who has been dead for forty-seven years. An hour later, the Saturday commanding officer misreads Coca's release order, and Coca is on the street twelve hours in advance of schedule. He walks home to Sherman Drive, on a bright, clear day of bracing air at fifty-two degrees—the best day of the week—strolling a meandering route, a seventy-five-minute journey, tapping his nose all the way with a splintered popsicle stick, muttering all the way. A passerby will eventually come forward to report to the police that Coca had stopped her with tears in his eyes, saying, "Mr. Capecelatro does not accept collect calls from jihadists."

COCA, 10:30 A.M.

Drives to the 7-Eleven on Eagle Street and purchases three twenty-five pound bags of ice.

CONTE AT HOME, 10:30 A.M.

Calls Catherine to tell her that her list of agencies was incomplete. His own Google search found one that Becky had surely dismissed because of its name: Rent a Wreck.

"Relax, Eliot. Bobby saw—did you forget? A late model, not a junker. Becky is a smart kid."

"But did she inquire? That's the question. I inquired. They rent two three-year-old vehicles, repainted, new tires, at rates the major agencies can't match because they deal strictly in new cars. A three-year-old model is easily mistaken for a new model—especially after you've been shot three times. This is not about Becky's intelligence. This is about a serious glitch in a case of multiple murders."

"Just say it: You want me to drive back to Syracuse and check this out."

"Before he's released sometime in the early evening. Please."

"I'll do it, but that's the end of this wild goose chase. I have a meeting with Don and Tino Mendoza in about an hour to review Barbone, Kovac, and Santoro. Then an appointment with Dr. Greenblatt at 1:30. Then I'll go."

"I'm not asking you to reschedule Greenblatt."

"I'm not asking you to get counseling."

"Promise you'll text me if you hit the jackpot. I'll be in Troy with Bobby and Maureen at *Trovatore*, starting at two until about five thirty."

CONTE AT HOME, 10:45 A.M.

Calls Antonio Robinson.

"Robby, me."

"Now what?"

"What are you doing today?"

"Slitting my wrists."

"Home all day?"

"What are you after, Eliot?"

"I'm making those special meatball sandwiches you love and inviting you to the *Trovatore* in Troy. Whaddya say we get those Saturday afternoons going again? Let's get back on track, bro."

(Silence.)

"Robby, you still there?"

"Whatever happened to us, El? It's been a year since we—what happened, El?"

"Never mind the past. It's now. We're now."

"The past, El. You can't just—"

"The music, Robby, on those Saturday afternoons? The wineskin of Chianti? The fabulous sandwiches? You could stop at The Florentine and pick up a half dozen cannolis. Come on! Whaddya say, Robby?"

"Just the two of us again?"

"Yeah, sure. I'll drive. Come over at noon, and that'll give us time to get there without breaking the speed limit."

He hangs up and calls Rintrona to give him the news that Antonio Robinson will be coming with him to the *Trovatore*, that he's making enough sandwiches for the four of them, and not to worry because Antonio is clean.

Rintrona says, "I'll be carrying just in case." Conte assures him that Robinson doesn't know who he is.

Rintrona asks, "That a fact because it better be," and Eliot lies again, "That's a fact. He has no idea."

Rintrona wants to know, "What's so important that you have to bring him of all people to this beautiful occasion?"

"Because he's my brother, Bobby, and I miss him."

"My heart goes fuckin' pitter-pat. What am I supposed to do? You claim he doesn't know me, but I know *him*. I witnessed him stone-cold execute that guy."

"What you do is call on your extensive experience as an actor with Troy Little Theater. We'll play it as it lays."

"Have any idea, Eliot, how long it's been since I've been laid?"

COCA AT HOME, 11–12 NOON

Vacuums and dusts. Shaves face, arms, chest, and legs. Flosses and brushes. Locates fedora at back of closet. Irons dark suit.

COCA AT HOME, 1 P.M.

Cleans and loads snub-nosed .38. Pours the three bags of ice into the claw-footed bathtub and runs cold water. Lowers himself in. Dozes.

GERALDINE WILLIAMS, 1:30 P.M.

Places in her Cadillac SUV three suitcases of clothes and one of firearms. At two she'll drive to 1318 Mary Street to find no one at home. She'll try again at 3:30 with the same result and will decide to return in the early evening before hitting the road for the long drive to Phoenix. She needs to talk to Conte about a business matter of mutual interest. And then perhaps … She's thinking around seven o'clock.

IN TROY

Noon: Antonio Robinson calls Conte to say that he'll take a rain check, maybe next week, he'd really like that, but he needs to spend the afternoon at the hospital with Milly. "I've been a lousy husband, El."

1:30: Catherine Cruz enters her medical clinic and is told that Dr. Greenblatt is running about an hour behind schedule. She decides to wait after calling Rent a Wreck and being informed that the agency will be open until seven.

2:30: At the funeral home on Rutger Street hosting the wake of Billy Santoro, a well-dressed man in a fedora enters, walks to the closed casket, kneels, and prays out loud three Hail Marys. Then rises and offers his condolences to Billy's relatives. Remo says to Gene, "I didn't know Coca knew Billy." Gene replies, "He didn't." Don says, "So what's he doing here? I don't like it."

At The Galaxy, Conte, Rintrona, and Maureen do not have time to eat the special meatball sandwiches before the gold curtain rises at the Met. They do so during the first intermission. They're happy. Verdi's impossible-to-follow libretto concerns them not. In *Il Trovatore*, Verdi's vocal writing was at its ravishing peak. So who cares what the story is? You want story? Read, as Rintrona put it during the first intermission, "a fuckin' novel." "The only problem," as Conte remarks to Rintrona and Maureen, "it takes the world's best singers to pull this opera off with full effect. Which today's cast certainly fills the bill." Rintrona says, "I don't even read the subtitles. Who gives a shit what they're sayin'?" Maureen says, "Enough with the language, Robert." "They open their mouths, Maureen, either sex, I want to jump in."

Near the end of act 3, when the tenor launches the opera's most famous aria, Maureen says, too loud, "Oh God! That's it! That's what I heard when Aida, oh God!" People in the vicinity turn in irritation. Rintrona elbows his wife. When the tenor launches the second verse, she jumps up, "Oh, God! When Aida!" She says, "I can't hold it any longer" and runs to the restroom. They follow her out as the curtain falls on act 3. Rintrona says, "We know now what we have to do. I'm going to ice this bastard."

4:45: Intermission nearing its end. No text yet from Catherine. Conte calls. She says, "I was about to text you. We've got him." He says, "Call Antonio, tell him to hold Coca on murder charges and get back to me on that right away." "I did. Couldn't get him. I'll try someone else." Maureen appears and Rintrona tells her to go home after it's over—he's got business with Eliot in Utica. Catherine calls back to tell Conte that Coca's been out since midmorning and Don Belmonte has been sent to Sherman Drive to pick him up. There's an all-points bulletin to all cruisers city- and countywide. "One more thing. In our meeting this morning, Tino Mendoza reported something about the Barbone case, which he doesn't understand and neither do I, but I have a feeling you might. I'll fill you in later."

5:35: The man in the fedora easily jimmies Conte's front door, goes in, turns on all the lights, closes the blinds of the large front window that gives onto the street.

5:45: The man in the fedora knocks on the door of Conte's next-door neighbors, the Morenos. Florencio opens the door, the man flashes a badge and is admitted. Ten minutes later, the three Morenos walk out with the man close behind, holding a revolver in the back of Angel Moreno. They enter Conte's house.

6:00: Geraldine Williams pulls to the curb at Conte's house. Is about to knock on the front door when a shot rings out from within. She retreats quickly to her SUV and removes from the suitcase of firearms the long-barreled .44 Magnum, silencer-equipped. Jogs up the driveway to the side of the house—a high window there without curtains or blinds. Too high for her to see inside. A second shot from within. Pulls the SUV alongside and climbs up onto its roof. Clear view of a couch. Three people seated. The boy is in the middle. The middle-aged man and woman on either side of him have been executed. Grievous head wounds. Blood on the walls. The man pats the boy on the head. Then sits in a chair opposite the window, in profound peace, closing his eyes. The man in the chair, still wearing his fedora, is not in a hurry. Because he has a plan. The best is yet to be. The woman on the roof of the SUV is a superb shot. Ordinarily, as on eleven previous occasions, she would do him with a single head shot. She believes he is certain to kill the boy. Should she miss, somehow, but how could Geraldine Williams miss? But if she should, he'd have a chance at the boy. She plays it safe with a blast midbody that penetrates his stomach and smashes all the way through to his spine, shattering it. His gun drops to the floor. Geraldine Williams jumps down from the roof of the SUV and karate kicks open the locked door as Conte and Rintrona arrive and the boy races screaming into the night and into the arms of Eliot Conte. Followed by Rintrona, he carries the boy in and is hit by the horror on the couch and Geraldine Williams holding the muzzle of her gun to Coca's head. Coca manages a smile and these words: "I was waiting … for Eliot to see his little … angel go to heaven … the best part." Geraldine Williams says, "I need to be alone with him for a moment. Take the boy, Mr. Conte, and your friend outside for a moment. I need a moment." They exit. When they reach the sidewalk, she comes to the threshold: "Okay. I've had my moment. His account is closed. I'm leaving my card on your desk should you wish, Mr. Conte, to engage me on what was too briefly discussed at Joey's. And a second card, which will put you in touch with intimate friends of mine in Philadelphia. Italians like you. They do cleanup of extreme scenes. Not a trace will remain."

SUNDAY, 12:30 A.M., CATHERINE'S APARTMENT

With Angel Moreno heavily sedated and asleep in the spare room, Catherine Cruz makes a light pasta sauce of garlic, sage, and olive oil. They eat in silence. Conte's not spoken a word for more than two hours. He speaks, "Great sauce, really great, but too late for the garlic to work."

She's puzzled.

"Too late to ward off evil."

She says, "Oh. Coffee?"

"Why not? I won't sleep anyway."

Over coffee, "Forgive me, Eliot, I can't turn off the detective in me. I'm curious about one last thing. Okay. Here it is: Doesn't matter, I suppose. He's dead, so it really doesn't matter, but my question is how did Coca know you and Bobby were his torturers if you were both disguised beyond recognition, as you told me, and he doesn't know Bobby from Adam, and you're silent through the entire event? Your theory that he went on a killing spree because of you assumes he knew you were involved in the torture. How could he possibly have known?"

"He did."

"How?"

"Somehow."

" 'Somehow' is where maybe Tino Mendoza comes in—you know Tino? I think you'd like him. An obsessive like your man Melville. Tino is a mess. Pretty much sleepless since Tuesday when he caught the Barbone murder. He goes back through a year and a half of Freddy's credit card receipts and sees that you, 'Mr. Johnnie Walker,' he says, purchased a bottle of Campari last October. He thinks this is strange because you're strictly a Johnnie Walker man, the receipts make that clear, two bottles per week. Sometimes three or four a week. He sees that Coca is a Campari man exclusively. He can't recall that many Campari buyers in the receipts, so he goes through them all again. Tino is relentless. You just once, Coca frequently, and only four others—that's it. Two are octogenarian women, who he eliminates as persons of interest. The other two are dead. He's intrigued that you bought Campari out of the blue, he says, and Don, who can't abide him—who never, by the way, shared the ballistics with Tino that link Barbone with the dog killing in Troy—which is wrong, I told Don, a professional scandal, I told him—Don says fuck that glory hound Mendoza, Catherine, I'll solve the Barbone case too—Don says to Tino, Why is this Campari crap important? What's your so-called point? Tino says back to him, You only know the point when you're almost at the point of an arrest. Until then, he says to Don, almost everything is pointless. I have nothing, he says, except those Campari receipts plus the fact that whoever did it was a known customer or Freddy doesn't open the door after closing. Conte and Coca are known customers, he says. I'm just reaching in the dark, he says, so I got in touch with Coca's wife."

"Denise."

" 'Because,' Tino says, 'no use talking to Coca, he's totally mental.' Do you know what Denise tells him? That just after Michael was released from the psychiatric ward last February, the first thing he says to her as she drives him home, which convinced her that he was not right yet, was that someone had tampered with his Campari and this someone was none other than you. He told her you drugged him. So she asks him, 'Why do you think Eliot would do such a terrible thing?' He told her that Freddy Barbone said that he, Michael, and you, Mr. Johnnie Walker Black himself, were now, in Freddy's words, 'both girlie men because you bought a bottle of Campari.' Now, of course, she thought he was nuts and Tino has no idea, *at this time*, he emphasizes, what the Campari connection really means, but he knows it has a meaning along with the fact of the broken Johnnie Walker bottle near Barbone's body, and he intends to question you, he says. Don told me after the meeting you had a thing for Denise and vice versa. Did anything go on? Jealousy a secret factor here? Don says Denise once told Millicent Robinson she had a dream about going to bed with you—this apparently got around. Maybe it got back to Michael? Maybe this is the motivation?"

"Nothing went on, believe me. I bought the Campari because I needed to experiment with it. My plan was to break into Coca's house while he's at work, lace the bottle with chloral hydrate—"

"What's that?"

"Something to knock him out so Bobby and I could do what we had to do. And did. I bought the Campari in order to determine if the color would change after I dosed it. It didn't."

"What exactly did you do to Coca?"

"The only other detail I'll ever give you, Catherine, is that as we brought him to consciousness we played at the highest volume the big tenor number from *Trovatore*. That's what he heard. Which is what Maureen heard when the dog was shot. She identified it today at The Galaxy. Geraldine Williams also heard something operatic when Kovac was killed, but she doesn't know opera."

"You think he had the bottle tested?"

"No, because we dumped the remaining contents in the toilet, which in retrospect wasn't smart. Because the bottle was three-quarters full when he took the drink that put him out. It was my one mistake. I should have brought an untampered bottle and exchanged it for the dosed one. He must have put it together. The drugging, the empty bottle, my girlie purchase, which Freddy alerted him to, and came up with—"

"You."

"Yes. That's how he must have made the connection. Someone tampered with his Campari, he speculates me, and he was right. Which is how all the violence began. I'm the cause. Never the target. He wanted a living death for me and he gets his wish. Michael Coca was waiting for me to come home in order to execute Angel in my presence. But he hadn't planned on Geraldine Williams because nobody can plan on Geraldine Williams. I tortured him, he tortured me. He won."

"But how do we explain why Bobby was hit first? How could Michael Coca have known Bobby was involved?"

"He may not have. We know that Coca, when he was assistant chief, had knowledge of the incident in Troy and that you and Bobby took me in. We also know Antonio was aware we'd been going down to Troy regularly to see the Rintronas. Did Antonio mention this to Milly? Who in turn mentions it to her best friend, Denise Coca? Who in turn lets it drop innocently to Michael? Who then concludes someone from out of town was my accomplice in his torture? That it was Bobby? Or is it enough that he knows Bobby and I are friends? Pointless speculation. Too many questions. Either way it comes back to me. Makes no difference."

She rises and walks over to Conte. He remains seated. Puts her hand on his shoulder, stroking it, "Angel is alive, El. He's going to need you." He looks up at her. Takes his hand and places it on her abdomen: "El, I'm pregnant."

CHAPTER 16

A week after the shootings on Mary Street, Antonio Robinson called a press conference. He connected the Barbone killing with the shootings in Troy and the murders of Florencio and Elvira Moreno. He spoke of ballistic evidence. He spoke of the car rental in Syracuse, which pointed, in his words, "almost definitively," to Michael Coca. " 'Almost' is the word," he said. Asked about motive, he said he would not speculate except to say that "insanity was a good guess." Asked about the shotgunning of Dragan Kovac and the deliberate hit-and-run killing of Billy Santoro, he said he had "nothing at this point." Asked about the killing of Coca himself, and the witness on Mary Street who "claimed" (Robinson's word) to have seen a black Cadillac SUV speeding away at the time of the killings, he replied that eyewitness accounts are notoriously unreliable, and at any rate this one was contradicted both by Eliot Conte and a detective from Troy, Robert Rintrona, who saw no such vehicle. Asked by a minor CNN producer (the events grazed the national media) to account for the difference in ballistics of the bullets that killed the Morenos and the single bullet that killed Coca, Robinson said the significance was obvious. Two different guns. When the producer said, "That certainly points to two different gunmen," Robinson responded, "Yes, it does, 'points' is the word, points, but we have no information at this time to pursue that possibility, strong as it seems," and referred the producer again to the testimony of Conte and Rintrona.

Three days later, CNN ran a story resuscitating the history of Utica in the 1950s, when major crimes, including Mafia hits, were blanketed by cover-ups assumed to be of political origin. The CNN segment concluded with noting ("We note, for what it's worth") that the witness on Mary Street given most credence by Utica's chief of police was "none other than the son of legendary upstate New York political boss Silvio Conte, and the Chief's oldest friend, a 'virtual brother,' many Uticans say. Just why the crazed killer chose to execute his last victims in the home of Eliot Conte is a question no Utican, not even Chief Robinson, is willing to address, not even anonymously."

Ten days after the shooting on Mary Street, Catherine takes Angel to his first therapy session, Conte sits alone nursing his manuscript on Melville, when the phone rings. An area code he does not recognize:

"Yes?"

"Professor Conte."

"Can it be you, Mirko?"

"It is."

"My God, Mirko, I'm so sorry—where are you? Will you return to Utica?"

"I will not."

"How can I help you? Please tell me."

"If you would be so kind, Professor Conte, to listen, this will be how you can help."

"I'm happy to listen—I don't mean I'm happy. I am not happy. I mean—"

"Sir, I understand your meaning. Thank you."

"May I ask if you are with Delores?"

"You may, but I'll not answer. What Mr. Martello said in his press conference. It is almost all true."

"Almost?"

"Our Imam is not in contact with radical clerics anywhere. This is true. My parents are innocent. This is true. There was no plot to do something terrible on Sunday. This is also true. He said Mirko Ivanovic is innocent. This is not true."

"What can that possibly mean? I don't believe it."

"The Imam was in communication with someone here. A citizen. A Bosnian Muslim living in Salt Lake City for many years as a Mormon. To do something not on Sunday, but on Monday."

"You knew about this?"

"Yes."

"You and the Imam were conspiring? Can this be true? What are you saying, Mirko?"

"I must confess all to you because I respect and I love you and cannot keep this thing inside me any longer. We had a plan to do something on Monday."

"What something?"

"Congressman Kingwood was to announce his bid for the Senate on Monday, at City Hall, at noon. At which time he would be assassinated."

(Silence.)

"Professor Conte, are you there?"

(Silence.)

"Professor, I think we have a phone problem."

"Are you the gentle Mirko who sat in my class on Hawthorne and Melville? You at least have his voice."

"We are not animals, sir. There never was a plan for a suicide bomb on Monday, if this is your thought, to slaughter the innocent. But then we heard that the announcement was moved to Tuesday, and to Kingwood's home, where he would be surrounded by his family and his dogs and bodyguards. Only TV cameras and two pool reporters permitted inside. At City Hall it was to be surgical—an up-close shooting of an evil man by a fake reporter with fake credentials, who would take his own life to ensure his lips would be forever sealed. There was no possibility to do this after the change of venue."

(Silence.)

"Professor Conte?"

"Why are you telling me that you conspired to do murder? Why would you tell anybody?"

"I do not tell just anybody. Only you."

"The Mirko I know—impossible."

"Two Muslims murdered in Phoenix, another castrated in Tucson, acid in the face for one in Dallas, a Muslim lady in New York City, in traditional dress, pushed onto the subway tracks, mangled beyond recognition. All in the last eighteen months, since Kingwood became chair of the House Committee on Homeland Security."

"What exactly was your role?"

"To bring the shooter an untraceable revolver."

"How did you acquire the weapon?"

"I will not tell you."

"What was the need for *you* to do that?"

"Very few are willing to do such a disgraceful thing."

"Couldn't the Imam have gotten someone else? Why you?"

"He trusted only me because he knew my views on Kingwood. We Muslims are decent, though I am not."

(Conte is silent.)

"Truthfully, Professor Conte, I wanted to be instrumental in the removal from life of the congressman."

"You speak of murder so matter-of-factly. This is not Mirko."

"Not matter-of-factly. My parents are dead, and I don't believe it was a double suicide. It was double murder caused by Kingwood. I'm a few days married and my grief makes me unreachable to my wife. She knows nothing of what I tell you. I am in ruins, Professor. I am slowly dying at a young age. You must now go to the police. Tell them I am in Louisville, Kentucky, at the YMCA and will stay until they arrest me. Please tell them. I accept your judgment. This city you would love, Professor Conte, so many parks, such greenery. Did the authorities look into the computer? Did I bring them to my parents and their death? I am responsible?"

"Your computer, you left it behind. Why?"

"It was not mine. It was the family computer. My e-mail was password protected. No documents in the hard drive, sir."

"Ah. I assure you it wouldn't have mattered if you'd taken it with you. Martello's people could easily hack your e-mail, and no doubt did. The other thing I can assure you of, had you succeeded in killing that bastard, you would've brought more anti-Muslim violence than we care to imagine. Nevertheless, an evil man, as you call him, and I agree, would've been removed from our midst. But now he's removed anyway. Legally. In either case, fuck him."

"You won't tell the authorities because you hate Kingwood too and wouldn't have shed a tear at his death?"

"I intend to keep your conspiracy to commit murder to myself. Were I still drinking, and had his assassination gone down, I'd lift a toast in celebration."

"We must not talk this way, Professor."

"I agree."

"It is unhealthy, Professor. A bad sign about us."

"I agree."

"You forgive me out of mutual hatred of Kingwood and the harm he does? Is this the reason?"

"Who am I to forgive anyone? I'll shield you from the police because I care for you as if you were my son. It's that simple in my moral universe."

"Then you are in danger too. You are complicitous."

"There are many ways to do the right thing, Mirko. This is my way."

"Like Mr. Melville's Ahab, we both hate evil."

"Mirko, Ahab was insane."

"Professor Conte, have we gone insane?"

"Without question. This is our bond."

SIX MONTHS LATER

Not once had the boy spoken since that night in December when his parents were shot to death as he sat between them on the couch in Conte's living room. The psychiatrist who'd secured him a leave for the second semester of his freshman year at Proctor High thought it a major step forward when, after three months of futile therapy, three sessions per week, she'd gotten him to write responses on a notepad. Mainly one word. Occasionally whole phrases. Finally, a week ago, a question: *What will become of me?* When she reminded him that Eliot Conte and Catherine Cruz were in the process of formally adopting him, he wrote: *But what will become of me?*

As Catherine grew big with child, she, Conte, and the boy lived in the first-floor apartment of the Morenos, amid the personal effects of the deceased—an unhealthy comfort for the boy, Conte knew, whom he'd witnessed too many times standing before the large front window of 1318 Mary, the scene of the crime, staring at the drawn blinds. Conte's old house, empty for six months, was on the market because he believed that he needed to move his new family, soon to be enhanced by a daughter in early August, out of lower East Utica, his heart's neighborhood, to where, exactly, he could not say and did not wish to contemplate. The guys at Toma's, of course, made many suggestions. Anthony Senzalma offered as a gift his fortress on Smith Hill, but Conte was not tempted by the isolation and silence up there and graciously refused, and Senzalma had responded, "I agree. No one should live like that. I, myself, can't anymore, which is why I shall move to the Presidential suite at Hotel Utica to brood upon my uncertain arrangements."

Conte had little time for brooding. His focus was on the boy and how to bring him, if possible, back to normal. He thought it might not be possible. So he took the boy with him to the class he was teaching for the spring semester on classic American fiction. The boy seemed disconnected until one evening he saw him open *The Adventures of Huckleberry Finn.* At two in the morning Conte awoke with the boy on his mind and saw the light still on in his room. And again at 4:30. At breakfast, the boy did not appear. When Conte checked on him, he saw that he was near the end of Twain's novel, where Huck says he's had it with civilization and will "light out for the territory." Was this Angel's desire too?

So he took the boy with him to Toma's on Tuesday mornings, without fail. In the beginning, the gang was intimidated by the boy's tragic presence and there was little of the old comic banter, but after a while the guys got their groove back and the talk of bodily ills resumed, in the usual witty style. After several of those Tuesdays at Toma's, Conte received a call from Gene who told him that he saw a quick, faint smile—it disappeared as soon as it appeared—as Angel listened attentively while Remo told the grievous tale of McLaine, whom he did not hesitate, though the man was long dead, to call, in the boy's presence, a cocksucker.

And Kyle Torvald saw the boy twice a week at POWER UP!, where he introduced him to what he called "the severe and only way to work out." The boy was skinny, Kyle said, but strong, pound for pound exceptionally strong. The boy threw himself with such scary abandon into the exercises that Kyle was worried.

And Antonio Robinson took him to spring training in Tampa to watch the Yankees. And Anthony Senzalma bought him an expensive laptop, in the $6,000 range, a hacker's delight, which Conte believed, but could not be certain, that Angel was beginning to use in recent weeks, in the middle of the night.

June 6, a perfect afternoon of late spring. They sit in the backyard at a round picnic table. The guests: Anthony Senzalma, Antonio Robinson, Kyle Torvald. Catherine has just returned from The Florentine with the extraordinary cake. She's decided against candles. It is Angel's fourteenth birthday. From the garage, Eliot hauls a potted sapling. Three feet tall. The day before, as Angel watched from his bedroom window, Conte dug the hole on the property line separating the Moreno yard from his. They sing Happy Birthday, softly. Conte takes the boy's hand and the guests follow him to the hole, Kyle carrying the potted sapling. Catherine lingers at the table.

In a voice no longer layered with the argot and tones of the boy that was, a voice painfully rough with disuse and not able to ascend above a whisper, Angel Moreno says, "The story you told me when I was six."

Conte says, "Yes."

Angel says, "It's a cherry tree?"

Conte says, "Yes," and removes the sapling from the pot, places it in the hole and offers the boy a shovel, who refuses it, goes down on his hands and knees and slowly pushes the dirt into the hole, patting and smoothing the last handfuls. Angel rises, wipes his hands on his jeans and shirt, wipes his hands on his face and says to Conte, "Thank you, sir." Catherine walks over. Angel puts his hand on her abdomen. He smiles, not big, but big enough, waiting for the kick within.

MELVILLE INTERNATIONAL CRIME

Happy Birthday, Turk!
Jakob Arjouni
978-1-935554-20-2

More Beer
Jakob Arjouni
978-1-935554-43-1

One Man, One Murder
Jakob Arjouni
978-1-935554-54-7

Kismet
Jakob Arjouni
978-1-935554-23-3

Brother Kemal
Jakob Arjouni
978-1-61219-275-8

The Craigslist Murders
Brenda Cullerton
978-1-61219-019-8

Death and the Penguin
Andrey Kurkov
978-1-935554-55-4

Penguin Lost
Andrey Kurkov
978-1-935554-56-1

The Case of the General's Thumb
Andrey Kurkov
978-1-61219-060-0

Nairobi Heat
Mukoma wa Ngugi
978-1-935554-64-6

Black Star Nairobi
Mukoma wa Ngugi
978-1-61219-210-9

Cut Throat Dog
Joshua Sobol
978-1-935554-21-9

Brenner and God
Wolf Haas
978-1-61219-113-3

The Bone Man
Wolf Haas
978-1-61219-169-0

Resurrection
Wolf Haas
978-1-61219-270-3

Come, Sweet Death!
Wolf Haas
978-1-61219-339-7

Murder in Memoriam
Didier Daeninckx
978-1-61219-146-1

A Very Profitable War
Didier Daeninckx
978-1-61219-184-3

Nazis in the Metro
Didier Daeninckx
978-1-61219-296-3

He Died with His Eyes Open
Derek Raymond
978-1-935554-57-8

The Devil's Home on Leave
Derek Raymond
978-1-935554-58-5

How the Dead Live
Derek Raymond
978-1-935554-59-2

I Was Dora Suarez
Derek Raymond
978-1-935554-60-8

Dead Man Upright
Derek Raymond
978-1-61219-062-4

The Angst-Ridden Executive
Manuel Vázquez Montalbán
978-1-61219-038-9

Murder in the Central Committee
Manuel Vázquez Montalbán
978-1-61219-036-5

The Buenos Aires Quintet
Manuel Vázquez Montalbán
978-1-61219-034-1

Off Side
Manuel Vázquez Montalbán
978-1-61219-115-7

Southern Seas
Manuel Vázquez Montalbán
978-1-61219-117-1

Tattoo
Manuel Vázquez Montalbán
978-1-61219-208-6

Death in Breslau
Marek Krajewski
978-1-61219-164-5

The End of the World in Breslau
Marek Krajewski
978-1-61219-274-1

Phantoms of Breslau
Marek Krajewski
978-1-61219-272-7

The Minotaur's Head
Marek Krajewski
978-1-61219-342-7

The Accidental Pallbearer
Frank Lentricchia
978-1-61219-171-3

The Dog Killer of Utica
Frank Lentricchia
978-1-61219-337-3